U0153464

凝煉知識品味閱讀

開口就會
英國長住用語
Live and Speak in Britain

周　樹　華◎著

五南圖書出版公司 印行

To the Reader 給讀者

本書獻給有興趣自學英語，旅居、留學或遊學英國的英語愛好者。透過本書提供的英國文化知識及真實英語情境對話，讀者可以在旅居或留學英國期間，順利融入英國生活環境，並與當地人士建立一些共同話題。旅居國外，語言能力固然重要，但擁有表達自己的文化，並了解對方文化的跨文化技能（intercultural skills）才是最重要的，所謂知己知彼，才能達到真正與人溝通的目的。

英語不是困難的語言，也不難學。考試、教學方式及錯誤的觀念（如說英語要有美國口音），造成我們學習英語的障礙。本書讀者會發現，閱讀英國報紙及英國電視節目中的對話，並不需要儲備一定的字彙量，也不應受到英語級數的限制。將字典下載到手機中，隨用隨查，這種學習的方便性，有助於讀者字彙量的快速增加及閱讀能力的提升。善用網路資源及手機，您可以成為一個獨立自主的英語學習者；而在文化認知上，則是「秀才不出門，能知／做天下事」。

本書呈現的情境對話，多是較長的對話，希望能引導讀者延伸思考問題；同一問題，也提供幾個不同的回答方式給讀者參考，這也比較符合現實生活中的「真實英語」（Authentic English）。尤其重要的是，簡短的情境對話，隱藏了文化內涵，讀者從中可以學到「怎麼說，說什麼」。

非常感謝五南出版社給我機會及充分的自由，不受任何英語級數、字彙多寡與題材的限制，依據個人旅居留學英國多年的切身經驗，及三十多年英語教學心得，寫一本英國文化與真實英語並重的讀本，與讀者分享。感謝朱曉蘋主編及吳雨潔編輯，她們的專業與努力，使本書順利出版。

臺灣大學外國語文學系退休副教授
英國曼徹斯特大學英國文學博士
周樹華

目錄

Unit 1 Housing 住所

Unit 2 The Press Media and Communications 平面媒體與通訊

Unit 3 Daily Life 日常生活

Unit 4 Transport 交通

Unit 5 Leisure Activities 休閒活動

Unit 6 Healthcare 醫療

Unit 7 Entertaining BBC TV Programmes BBC 有趣的電視節目

Unit 8 Understanding Advertising 閱讀廣告

Appendixes 附錄

Unit 1 Housing

住所

旅居英國購屋、租房不求人需具備對英國「住」的基本知識及英語表達能力。國情不同買房租屋規定也不同，如：購買不動產律師的職責、房屋類型的描述、租屋法規、搬家費用等。了解這些差異，按部就班遵守規定，必可順利找到理想的居住環境。另外，旅居他國也應有環保意識，因此在資源回收部分，讀者會認識許多住家垃圾分類與資源回收的英語單詞。利用本單元提供的實用語句，必可達到與房屋仲介充分溝通的目的。

1.1 Property Seeking 購屋

在英國買房、租房的信息有很多管道，讀者可在當地的房屋仲介公司（estate agents）、地方報紙（local papers），商店窗戶貼有租屋廣告（shop windows），尋找適合的住處。但最方便的就是利用網站。英國最大、最優質可信賴購屋、租屋的網站是 www.rightmove.co.uk，聰明的讀者，秀才不出門，能知英國房事，可在網上虛擬網購一番。

A: What can we help you find today?

A: 您在找什麼樣的房子呢？

B: Basically, we're looking for more space, so a detached house.

B: 我們需要更多空間，所以想找一間獨棟房屋。

A: So how many bedrooms would you need?

A: 要幾間臥室呢？

B: Preferably three.

B: 最好有3間臥室。

A: And what price range are you thinking of ? The average price for a detached property in Staffordshire is £280,000. This one has three bedrooms, a private garden and a conservatory.

A: 您可以接受什麼樣的價位呢？Staffordshire 地區的獨棟房屋平均價位約在 28 萬英鎊。例如這一棟，有 3 間臥室、私有花園及溫室。

B: What is the asking price?

B: 對方開價多少？

A: Are you a cash buyer? The asking price is £295,000.

A: 你付現金嗎？目前的要價是29萬5000英鎊。

B: Is there a chain?

B: 是否可以立即成交？

A: No, there is no chain.

A: 可以的。

B: Can we arrange a viewing, please?

B: 可以安排時間參觀嗎？

A: Certainly. Let me take down your details first.

A: 當然可以。請先給我您的聯絡資料。

A: How do I make an offer?	**A:** 我如何出價？
B: You can make your offer over the phone or in person. You should always follow up with an email so it is in writing.	**B:** 你可以打電話或當面出價。但接著要寫 email 留下文字紀錄。
A: They accepted my offer, what do I do next?	**A:** 出價接受後，下一步做什麼？
B: Once your offer has been accepted, it must be made in writing.	**B:** 出價被接受後，一定要有文字紀錄。
A: Should I order a survey?	**A:** 我需要替購買的房屋做鑑定嗎？
B: Yes, you should book a survey. The cheapest for the home condition report is about £250.	**B:** 是的，應該安排做鑑定。最便宜的房屋狀況報告大約要 250 英鎊。
A: How do I find a surveyor?	**A:** 到哪裡找一位鑑定員？
B: Your mortgage lender may suggest a company. Check that the surveyor is registered.	**B:** 貸款給你的人會推薦一間公司。查一下鑑定員是註冊合格的。

A: What do I do with survey results?

A: 鑑定結果有何用途？

B: Ideally, the property will get the thumbs up.

B: 理想而言，房屋會得到滿意的評價。

A: What about the legal side of things?

A: 法律部分如何處理？

B: Once your offer is accepted, you will need a solicitor to deal with the legal transfer of home ownership.

B: 對方接受你的出價後，你需要律師為你處理合法產權轉移。

A: So what do you think of the house?

A: 你看這房子如何？

B: It's fantastic! It needs a lot of doing to it, though.

B: 太棒了！但翻修的工程蠻大。

A: What do you think of the colour scheme?

A: 你覺得色調搭配如何？

B: It's too dark. We could do something brighter. We could go for cream or white.

B: 太暗了。我們可以用亮一點的顏色。用乳白色或白色。

A: Maybe. What about the kitchen?

A: 也行。廚房呢？

B: We could have an open plan kitchen. We could go and get a whole new kitchen.

B: 我們可以改成開放式廚房。我們可以換一整套全新的廚房。

A: That's wonderful!

A: 那真是太好了！

1. 我在找一間公寓／一房公寓／套房／雙拼獨棟／獨棟房屋／並排房屋／鄉間小屋／獨棟平房。
   I'm looking for a flat / a one-bedroom flat / a studio flat / a semi-detached house / a detached house / a terraced house / a cottage / a bungalow.
2. 房租多少？
   How much is the rent?
3. 已經有別人出價了嗎？
   Have other offers been made?
4. 可以議價嗎？
   Is the price negotiable?
5. 這個房子待售多久了？
   How long has it been on the market?
6. 附近有學校／小學／中學嗎？
   Is there a school / primary school / secondary school nearby?
7. 附近有商店嗎？
   Are there any local shops?
8. 停車如何安排？
   What are the car parking arrangements?

9. 有什麼樣的景觀呢？

What sort of view does it have?

10.是一樓嗎？（註：英國一樓是 ground floor，二樓是 first floor 等。）

Is it on the ground floor?

11.可以養寵物嗎？

Are pets allowed?

12.我想看看這戶房屋。

I'd like to have a look at this property.

13.我願意出價。

I'd like to make an offer.

14.你需要哪種類型的住處？

What kind of accommodation are you looking for?

15.你想要買還是租？

Are you looking to buy or to rent?

16.你要新式的還是老房屋？

Do you want a modern or an old property?

17.你需要院子 / 車庫 / 停車位嗎？

Do you want a garden / a garage / a parking space?

18.你有房子要賣嗎？

Have you got a property to sell?

19.你的預算是多少？

What's your budget?

20.你打算付什麼樣的價錢？

How much are you prepared to pay?

21.你可以接受什麼樣的價位？

What price range are you thinking of ?

22.每月租金需預付。

The rent's payable monthly in advance.

23.房屋的抵押金是一個月的房租。

There is a deposit of one month's rent.

24.你多快可以搬入？

How soon would you be able to move in?

25.你願意收到我們的資訊嗎？

Do you want us to put you on our mailing list?

◆ **待售或出租的房屋外面，通常會掛著房地產公司的牌子。**

For Sale	售
To Let	租
Under Offer	議價中
Sold	售出
Reduced	減價
New Price	新價
Offers around £250,000	開價 25 萬英鎊
Offers in excess of £180,000	出價超過 18 萬英鎊
£110 pw (per week)	週租 110 英鎊
£400 pcm (per calendar month)	月租 400 英鎊

英國房屋仲介公司網站中，對出售或出租的房屋，皆有詳盡的文字描述、圖片、街景圖，使用的字彙及句子都很固定，讀者只需閱讀一兩個具有代表性的例子，就能理解內容，挑選符合自己需求的房屋。

✲ 物件一

1 Key features 主要特色：

Private Garden Flat 有私人院子的公寓

Own Front Door 獨立進出

Bright and Spacious 明亮寬敞

Part Furnished 附部分家具

Available Now! 可立即入住

2 Full description 完整描述：

Large 1 double bedroom ground floor flat with private garden. Benefitting from own front door, bright and spacious living room, separate fully fitted kitchen, bathroom with shower and ideal for West Norwood station.

大空間的一樓公寓，包括一間雙人房及私人花園。專用前門方便獨立進出，客廳明亮寬敞，分隔的廚房設備完善，浴室設有淋浴。近 West Norwood 車站。

✲ 物件二

1 Key features 主要特色：

Beautiful Three Bedroom Property 美麗的三房住宅
Master Bedroom with En Suite 主臥室含一套衛浴
Open Plan Kitchen and Dining Room 開放式廚房及餐廳
Spacious Reception Room 寬敞客廳
Driveway 車道

2 Full description 完整描述：

A traditional three bedroom semi-detached property situated on an idyllic tree-lined road within Chorlton. The property is situated in close proximity to the main transport links. The property does require some updating and modernisation. This property comprises of an entrance hallway, two reception rooms, a kitchen, three bedrooms and a bathroom. The property is double glazed and has a fantastic southerly facing rear garden. No Chain. Ideal for those buyers who want to modernise a property to make it their own.

傳統雙拼獨棟三房住宅，位於 Chorton 市區內一條富田園風情的綠蔭路上，臨近主要交通接駁系統。必須進行部分改裝工程適應現代化居家環境。屋內格局包括廳門、兩間客廳、一間廚房、三間臥房、一間浴室。全屋已裝有雙層玻璃窗戶。漂亮的面南後花園是一大特色。可立即交屋。適合有興趣進行改裝更新工程，打造屬於個人特色的買主。

房子買定後，搬家應注意事項：

Timing: When planning your moving date, try to have at least a week's overlap.

安排時間：計畫搬家日期，最好多空出一週的時間。

Removals: Ask for personal recommendations and check the price includes insurance. Fridays aren't the best choice, as they are busy.
搬家：找有人推薦的搬家公司，查看保險費是否包括在內。週五不是最佳的選擇，因為他們較忙。

Packing: Try daypack.co.uk and helpineedboxes.co.uk
打包：建議用這兩個網站：daypack.co.uk 及 helpineedboxes.co.uk

Services: Two days before you move, let your electricity, gas and water suppliers know.
水電瓦斯業務：搬家前兩天，通知水、電、瓦斯供應公司。

Get connected: Find out who the phone, television and internet service providers are, and decide if you want to keep them on.
連線：找出新居的電話、電視及網際網路服務供應商，決定是否繼續使用。

Security: Decide if you are going to keep all the locks and security systems in place.
安全設備：決定是否要用現有的門鎖及安全系統。

Post: Have your mail redirected from your old address, at least for three months. royalmail.com/redirection
信件：可向郵局申請至少 3 個月內，將信件轉寄到新地址。

Be a good neighbour: Warn your neighbours about your move and check there will be space for the removal vans to park.
做個好鄰居：事先跟鄰居打招呼，告知搬家，並確定搬運車有地方停靠。

3 買房總花費

Here is a guide to the typical costs associated with buying a property worth £200,000.
依據 2013/09/01 *The Sunday Times* 提供的資料，買一戶價值 20 萬英鎊的房子，總共需要的費用。

Deposit: The bigger the better, but you'll generally need at least 10%.
自備款：愈多愈好，至少 10%。

Mortgage arrangement fee: For a £200,000 home, you'd be looking at about £300.

房貸費用：一戶 20 萬英鎊的房屋，需要 300 英鎊。

Services: This involves your solicitor going to the council to check whether there are planning or local issues that could affect the property's value. The price includes a drains search. £250-£300.

服務費：你的律師需要去市政府，查看有無影響房價的因素，包括檢查下水道。250 到 300 英鎊。

Legal costs: These will be £500-£750 depending on the value of the property and where you live. But for a £200,000 property house, you'd be looking at £500.

法律事務費：依據房屋的價格及地點，大約需要 500 英鎊到 750 英鎊。一棟價值 20 萬英鎊的房屋，需要 500 英鎊。

Stamp duty: The rate increases with the purchase price. For a £200,000 property house, you'll be looking at £2000.

印花稅：印花稅會跟著房價上漲。20 萬英鎊的房屋，需要 2000 英鎊。

Survey: A home condition survey costs about £250, a homebuyer's report about £400.

房屋鑑定費：房屋狀況鑑定費約 250 英鎊，但購屋人做的鑑定報告需 400 英鎊。

Moving costs: Budget for £300-£600.

搬家費：300 到 600 英鎊的預算。

Total: £23,949-£26,650.

總共花費：23,949 英鎊到 26,650 英鎊。

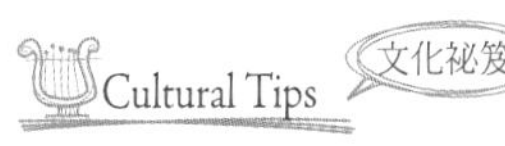

在英國買房有兩個關鍵字需要說明：

1. survey 英國出售房屋都會有一份房屋鑑定員（surveyor）針對房屋的結構、坪數大小、各種管線的安全、供暖及熱水系統、室內裝潢等，做出的專業鑑定報告。這份報告會影響房屋的價格。購屋人爲確保沒有買到有瑕疵的房屋，也會自己花錢找鑑定員，做詳盡的評估。
2. chain 這是英國房地產特有的現象，也是我認爲在英國購屋最關鍵並需要了解的資訊。一般英國人沒有很多現金，因此要先賣掉自己現有的房屋，才有財力換新房。每一戶要賣的房子都有一個賣方及買方，形成一連串的購屋鏈（chain），有時這個購屋鏈可以從南到北，遍及全英國。唯有一戶成交，在鏈子上的其他賣、買雙方才能被鬆綁，開始進行交易，進而解除這個購屋鏈。若是大家都無法成交，所有的賣主買主就會被鎖在鏈子上。因此，急於買屋的人，第一件事就必須詢問：'Is there a chain?' 如果沒有，交易過程即很單純，只要買賣方談好便可立即成交。

1.2 Renting a House 租房

英國是個講究法律的國家，租房、買房需經由律師（solicitor），依據合約行事。租房買房可尋求仲介公司（estate agency）的協助，他們負責提供顧客相關資料。租屋者付給仲介公司的費用包括：查核資料（checking references），提供財產清單（providing inventory），交付鑰匙（handling keys），電話往來與郵資（phone calls and postage），也需注意有續約費（renewal fees）及延遲付租罰金（late payment fees）。這些費用加起來並不便宜，因此必須要找可靠的仲介公司，先確定需要付的仲介費用。租房時還需付押金（deposit），通常是一個月的房租。租房、買房都有固定的英語表達方式，讀者只要認識一些基本的單字，了解租房需要問的問題，就可以溝通無虞。

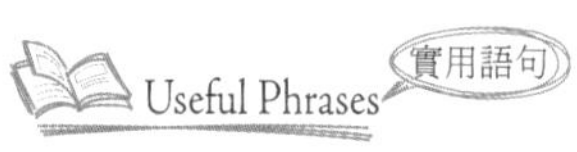

1. 租金多少？

How much is the rent?

2. 押金多少？
How much is the deposit?
3. 需要事先付租金嗎？
Do I need to pay rent in advance?
4. 收回押金的條件是什麼？
What are the conditions for getting my deposit back?
5. 冬天房子的暖氣費是多少？
How much does it cost to heat the house in winter?
6. 熱水及淋浴設備如何？
How do the hot water and shower work?
7. 這個地區安全嗎？
Is it a safe area?
8. 房屋有煙霧警報器及安全門嗎？
Does the house have smoke alarms and a fire escape?
9. 朋友可以來住嗎？
Can I have friends staying over?

1 Don't ignore the small print 留意合約中的小字細節

Make sure you're clear about what kind of tenancy agreement you're signing. Check the agreement includes all the relevant information, such as what the rent covers (does it include bills?), whether you can leave before the end of the tenancy and how much notice you have to give, and any rules on things like pets, guests and smoking. 你必須清楚了解所簽的租約內容。仔細檢查有沒有涵蓋所有相關細節：如租金是否包括水電費；若可以提前解約，需要多久之前通知房東；有關飼養寵物、訪客借住、吸菸等的規定。

2 Make sure the inventory is accurate 確定財物清單無誤

The inventory is a list of everything that's provided with the property, including furniture, carpets, curtains, appliances, crockery and cutlery. It should also record the condition everything is in – for example, existing damage or wear, such as an old stain on the carpet. Always make sure you are provided with an inventory – ask for one if necessary. If you're not given one, write one up yourself, get it signed by an independent witness and send a copy to the landlord. 財物清單詳列房屋內的家具、地毯、窗簾、家電、碗盤餐具。也記錄了房屋及物品的狀況、已有的破損，如地毯上的污漬。務必向房東或仲介公司索取財物清單，或自己列一份，在第三者見證簽字後，副本給房東。

3 Remember the bills 記住所有帳單

Don't forget to factor in costs on top of the rent, such as utility bills, TV licence and internet access costs. Watch out for any funny business with utility bills. 租房除了考慮租金，也別忘記算上水電、電視執照、網路等費用。尤其要注意水電帳單有無異常。

4 Safety, security and insurance 租屋安全及保險

Make sure all gas appliances have been checked by an engineer. And at least one smoke alarm should be fitted. 所有的瓦斯設備需經由專業人士檢查確認安全。屋內應該安裝至少一個煙霧警報器。

5 When it's time to leave ... 退租離開時

At the end of the tenancy you should get your deposit back within 10 days. Your landlord can't keep your deposit because of 'general wear and tear'. For example, if the carpet gets a bit worn out, it's probably wear and tear, but if you burn a hole in it, it's damage. 租約到期後，房東在十天內退還押金。房屋在正常使用下的耗損，並不構成扣押金的理由。舉例來說，地毯磨舊了屬於正常使用的耗損，但如果燒出一個洞，則算是破壞。

Inventory 租屋財物清單

從租屋財物清單中，讀者可清楚了解英國一般房屋的格局：如 living room（客廳），hallway（門廳），stairs（樓梯），kitchen and dining area（廚房及餐廳），bathroom（浴室），bedrooms（臥室），及每個房間所放置的家具及物品。房屋租妥後，一定要與房東一一核對清單，增減不在清單內的東西，退租時以此爲依據，不必負任何賠償責任。

特別需要注意的是：不要隨便清理貯藏雜物的車庫或屋頂閣樓，因爲很多看起來陳舊，看似可以丟棄的東西，可能是英國人的傳家之寶（雖然不一定値錢）。閱讀這份租屋家具設備清單，讀者不但學到日常生活中經常使用字彙，同時也認識英國人家中擺設的文化層面，是一舉兩得的英語學習材料。

Living Area 客廳

Item 名稱	Quantity 數量	Condition 狀況
Sofa 沙發		
Armchair 安樂椅		
Coffee table 咖啡桌		
Lamps 落地燈		
Curtains 窗簾		
Carpets 地毯		
Window fixtures 窗戶裝置		
Other 其他		
General condition of paint-work/paper 油漆及壁紙狀況		

Hallway and Stairways 門廳及樓梯

Item 名稱	Quantity 數量	Condition 狀況
Curtains 窗簾		
Carpets 地毯		
Other 其他		
General condition of paint-work/paper 油漆及壁紙狀況		

Kitchen / Dining Area 廚房 / 餐廳

Item 名稱	Quantity 數量	Condition 狀況
Cooker and Oven 炊具及烤箱		
Fridge 冰箱		
Microwave 微波爐		
Washing machine / tumble dryer 洗衣機 / 烘乾機		
Pots and pans 鍋具		
Crockery 碗盤		
Cutlery 刀叉		
Dining table and chairs 餐桌、椅子		
Flooring 地板		
Curtains / Window covers 窗簾及遮窗布		
Other 其他		
General condition of paint-work / paper 油漆及壁紙狀況		

Bathroom 浴室

Item 名稱	Quantity 數量	Condition 狀況
Bath / Shower 浴缸 / 淋浴間		
Toilet 馬桶		
Sink 洗臉槽		
Other 其他		
General condition of paint-work / paper 油漆及壁紙狀況		

Bedrooms 臥室

Item 名稱	Quantity 數量	Condition 狀況
Beds 床		
Wardrobe 衣櫥		
Chest of drawers 五斗櫃		
Bedside table 床頭櫃		
Lighting fixtures 燈具		
Other 其他		
General condition of paint-work/paper 油漆及壁紙狀況		

清單最後附上雙方聲明，簽名後開始生效。

This property has been fully inspected by both landlord / tenant and this inventory represents an accurate record of the state of repairs of this property on the date on which the tenants took over occupation. At the end of the tenancy, this inventory shall be used to assess the condition of the property. 本房屋經由出租人及承租人雙方徹底檢查，本財物清單是承租人租房日起的房屋及修

補狀況的正確記錄。租約結束，本清單將做爲評估房屋狀況的依據。

Signed（簽名）：
（Landlord 出租人）＿＿＿＿＿＿＿ Date：＿＿＿＿＿＿＿
（Tenant 承租人）＿＿＿＿＿＿＿ Date：＿＿＿＿＿＿＿

租房信件範本

租房能夠與房東相安無事，是最上策。萬一與房東發生任何糾紛，通常需要信件來往，文字爲憑。在此提供讀者兩封信件範本，內容簡單扼要，讀者只要學會正確的措辭用語，套入相關資料，就可以寫一封英文信了。

(1) Deposit Dispute 押金被扣的爭議

Dear XXX,

I am a former tenant of yours at XXX.

You have decided to retain £XXX of my security deposit. Can you please write to me, explaining the deductions which you feel entitled to make and enclosing copies of receipts to prove your expenditure on these items? I would appreciate it if you would respond to this letter by .

You can contact me to discuss this issue using the following contact information: ＿＿＿＿＿＿＿＿

Tenant(s) XXX

XXX：

我是曾住在＿＿＿的承租人。你已決定保留我的押金。請寫信告知你扣款的原因，並附上花費項目的收據。請在＿＿＿（日期）之前回覆此信，不勝感激。你可以透過這個信息＿＿＿跟我聯絡，並討論相關事宜。

承租人＿＿＿

(2) Arranging Repairs 安排修繕工程

Dear XXX,

I would like to draw your attention to repairs which need to be carried out at XXX

I would appreciate it if you could arrange to visit the property to inspect the following items and arrange for their repair.

Please contact me to discuss a suitable time for you to visit to carry out these inspections and repairs.

Tenant(s) XXX

XXX：

提醒您處理有關位於______的房屋修繕工程。假如您能前來查看並安排需要修理的項目，則不勝感激。請聯絡我，商量適當來訪時間，並進行檢查修理工作。

承租人______

1.3 Recycle 回收

全球環保運動最重要的項目之一就是回收（recycle）。現在無論居住何處，都要先了解並配合當地垃圾回收規定。英國每個城市的市政府（City Council）網站都有垃圾回收的資訊。市政府提供不同顏色的垃圾桶（bin）給住戶，住戶照規定分類，將垃圾桶放在戶外，市政府的垃圾車會按時收垃圾及回收物，也會按時清潔美容垃圾桶（bin beauty）。從市政府規劃的回收項目，我們可了解英國環保概念、垃圾分類及資源回收政策。讀者會發現英國人愛園藝，因此多一個綠色回收桶（Green-it bin），專收花園廢棄物（garden waste）。讀者只要閱讀有關垃圾回收的情境對話，就學到與資源回收相關的英語字彙。

A: When will my bin be collected?

A: 何時回收垃圾？

B: Your blue bin is collected every fortnight, on the same day as your household waste.

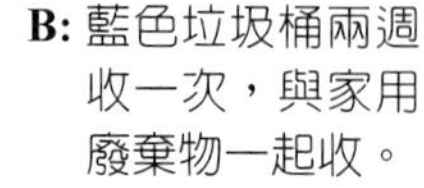

B: 藍色垃圾桶兩週收一次，與家用廢棄物一起收。

A: When do I put my bin out?

A: 何時將垃圾桶放在戶外？

B: Bins should be put out by 7:30 am on your collection day.

B: 收垃圾當天早上7:30。

A: What can I put in my blue recycle bin?

A: 藍色資源回收垃圾桶內放什麼？

B: Your blue bin makes it easier to recycle a wide range of items. Please only put the correct items in your recycling bin.

B: 藍色垃圾桶很容易回收很多東西。請只放正確的東西在內。

A: What should I not put in the recycle bin?

A: 回收桶不應放的東西是什麼？

B: Windowpanes, cookware, plastic bags, food trays, plastic films, cling film, foil, food waste, general waste.

B: 窗框、廚房用具、塑膠袋、托盤、塑膠膜、保鮮膜、錫箔紙、廚餘、一般垃圾。

Dialogue 2 對話2

A: When do I put my green bin out?

A: 何時將綠色垃圾桶放在戶外？

B: Bins should be put out by 7:30 am on your collection day.

B: 回收當日早上7:30將垃圾桶放在戶外。

A: What can go in the bin?

A: 垃圾桶內放什麼？

B: Green-it bin is a garden waste recycling service to turn your unwanted grass cuttings, leaves and pruning into something useful.

B: 綠色桶是花園廢物回收服務，可將不要的雜草、樹葉，整理成有用的東西。

A: Do I need to bag my garden waste?

A: 我需要將花園廢棄物放在袋子內嗎？

B: Please do not wrap/bag your garden waste before putting it in the bin. Make sure your loose garden waste is contained in the bin with the lid closed.

B: 請不要將花園廢棄物包起來放入垃圾桶內。只要將廢棄物放在桶內蓋上蓋子即可。

A: What should I not put in the Green-it bin?

A: 綠色回收桶不可放什麼？

B: Please do not place any of the following items in your Green-it bin: food waste, turf, soil, stones, flower pots and seed trays, any plastics, pet fouling, cat litter, nappies, vacuum cleaner contents, large branches, metals, glass, paper, cardboard, timber, planks of wood, general household waste.

B: 廚餘、草皮、土、石頭、花盆、種子盒、任何塑膠物、寵物大便、貓砂、尿布、吸塵器內廢物、大樹枝、金屬、玻璃、紙、硬紙箱、木材、厚木板、一般垃圾。

A: When will my household waste bin be collected?

A: 何時收家用廢棄物垃圾？

B: Your household waste bin is collected fortnightly.

B: 家用垃圾桶是兩週收一次。

A: What can I put in my household waste bin?

A: 家用垃圾桶內可放什麼？

B: Your household bin is for household and food waste, and items which cannot be recycled.

B: 家用垃圾桶僅放家用垃圾及廚餘，以及無法回收的東西。

A: What if my bin is not big enough?

A: 垃圾桶不夠大怎麼辦？

B: Double check if it can be recycled in your blue bin. You can also take the rubbish to one of our Household Waste and Recycling Centres.

B: 先查看有沒有東西可以放進藍色回收桶中。你也可以將垃圾送到我們的家用廢棄物及回收中心。

A: Can I replace my bin?

A: 我可以更換垃圾桶嗎？

B: Replacement bins can be ordered. There is a charge of £15 towards the cost of the replacement bin.

B: 可申請更換垃圾桶。需付 15 英鎊更換費。

In the inner box	回收桶內盒
Newspapers & magazines paper	報紙及雜誌
telephone directories	電話簿
white envelopes	白色信封
catalogues	目錄
In the main part of the recycling bin	回收桶內
plastic yoghurt pots	養樂多塑膠盒
plastic margarine and butter tubs	奶油塑膠盒
plastic cups	塑膠杯
juice cartons	果汁盒
cardboard	硬紙箱

plastic bottles (milk, water, shampoo, etc)	塑膠瓶（如牛奶、水、洗髮精等的容器）
cans	鐵罐
glass bottle and jars	玻璃瓶及玻璃罐

1.4 Utilities 水電

A: Hello, I am from British Gas. I'd like to read your gas meter.	**A:** 我是大英瓦斯。我來抄表。
B: Sorry, I don't understand.	**B:** 對不起。我不懂。
A: I need to take the reading of your electricity for the bill.	**A:** 我需要抄電表，核算電費。
B: Do I pay you?	**B:** 費用交給你嗎？
A: No, you get the electricity bill in the post.	**A:** 不，帳單會寄給你。
B: What do I do when I get the bill?	**B:** 收到帳單之後呢？
A: You pay through your bank. You can also use the internet.	**A:** 你從銀行付款。你也可以上網付款。

A: Hello. This is Mr. Taylor from JP Plumber. What is wrong?

A: 我是 JP Plumber 公司的泰勒。有何問題？

B: Our washing machine was broken. Could you fix it?

B: 洗衣機壞了。能修嗎？

A: I'll contact a plumber. But it'll probably be next week.

A: 我會聯繫水電工。但可能要下週。

B: But we need someone right now.

B: 但我們立刻要修。

A: Well, I'll try and get you a plumber ASAP.

A: 我看看能不能立刻找到一位水電工。

B: Sorry, ASAP?

B: 對不起，ASAP 是什麼意思？

A: Ah, as soon as possible.

A: 是立刻的縮寫。

Dialogue 3 對話3

A: Hello, it's the plumber here. What's the problem?

A: 我是水電工。有何問題？

B: My washing machine is leaking.	**B:** 我的洗衣機漏水。
A: I am sure I can help but I am tied up all morning.	**A:** 我一定可以幫忙，但早上已排滿。
B: What time can you come?	**B:** 你何時可以來？
A: I can come to your house and see your washing machine between half twelve and one.	**A:** 我大約十二點半到一點之間，到府上檢查你的洗衣機。
B: Thank you.	**B:** 謝啦。

Unit 2 The Press Media and Communications
平面媒體與通訊

無論是長住英國或短期旅居，我強力推薦大家多多接觸並利用英國高水準的媒體，如報紙、廣播、電視 BBC（British Broadcasting Corporation），增進英語聽、說、讀的能力；而要了解一個國家的文化特色，透過媒體當然是最直接有效的途徑。

本章節會提供一些摘自報紙的資料，幫助讀者熟悉媒體常用英語。讀者將會發現，其實報紙的英語，並沒有那麼難。

2.1 The British Newspapers 英國報紙

A: Which newspapers do you buy every day?

A: 你每天買什麼報紙？

B: I must confess I don't buy a newspaper every day. When I do buy one, it tends to be the *The Guardian*.

B: 說實話我沒有每天買報紙。要買一份的話，應該是《衛報》。

A: What do you like about the newspaper you read?

A: 你喜歡報紙的哪一點？

B: It is well written. It also has a crossword that is exactly the right level for me.

B: 文章寫的好。報紙上的填字遊戲適合我的程度。

A: Which newspapers do you read every day?

A: 你每天看什麼報？

B: I get *The Independent* every day, and *The Observer* on Sundays.

B: 我每天看《獨立報》，週日看《觀察家報》。

A: What do you like about them?

A: 你為何喜歡它們？

B: They are the only newspapers I trust. They seem impartial. They have interesting sections. *The Independent* has good coverage of the arts – exhibitions, shows, concerts, reviews.

B: 我只相信這兩份報紙。他們報導公正，有趣的版面。《獨立報》的藝術報導很好——有展覽、表演、音樂會、評論。

A: Which newspapers do you get?

A: 你買什麼報？

B: I get *The Mail*.

B: 我買《郵報》。

A: Why do you like to read it?

A: 你為何喜歡看？

B: It's pretty light-weight and readable. I don't like politics. *The Mail* has articles on health, fashion, film stars, diets.

B: 它讀起來很輕鬆。我不喜歡政治。《郵報》有與健康、時尚、影星、飲食相關的文章。

英國平面媒體以性質區隔，報紙可分爲 Broadsheet 及 Tabloid 兩大類。Broadsheet 及 Tabloid 中文找不到一個對等的翻譯，只能就報紙開數大小分別譯成「大報」（17×22 英寸）及「小報」（11×17 英寸）。但自 2004 年起，各大報紛紛進行改版，如 *The Independent*《獨立報》、*The Times*《泰晤士報》皆改成跟 Tabloid 開數相同的版面，但自稱爲 compact format（小型版）與小報做區隔。不過，《泰晤士報》的週日版 *The Sunday Times* 仍然維持 Broadsheet 大開數版面。*The Guardian*《衛報》於 2005 年改爲 12.4×18.5 英寸的 Berliner format，大小介於 Broadsheet 與 Tabloid 之間，比前者窄又比後者長。

英國報紙紙張大小，其實不單是版面的問題。Broadsheet 及 Tabloid 不同的新聞報導風格與讀者群的身分、教育程度、職業有密不可分的關係。看 Broadsheets 的讀者多爲受過高等教育的知識分子（well-educated intellectuals），屬於中產階級（middle class），擁有收入不錯的職業。而 Tabloids 的讀者多半僅受過義務教育（至 16 歲），多爲勞工階級（working class）的男士。因此報紙讀者群的背景，也充分反映出 Broadsheets 及 Tabloids 兩種報紙的差異，在此替讀者做一簡單說明。

英國報紙分類

The Broadsheets vs.The Tabloids 大報與小報	The Broadsheets = 口碑媒體（quality press）、重量級（heavyweight） *The Guardian*《衛報》 *The Times*《泰晤士報》 *The Daily Telegraph*《每日電訊報》 *The Independent*《獨立報》	The Tabloids = 迎合大衆的媒體（popular press） *The Sun*《太陽報》 *The Daily Mail*《每日郵報》 *The Mirror*《鏡報》 *The Star*《星報》

新聞報導內容	-Intensive coverage of national news and politics 深入報導全國性新聞及政治議題 -In-depth features on business, the arts, sport, science, the environment 針對財經、藝術、體育、科學、環境等議題的深入專題報導 -Background information on important events 重要事件提供背景資訊 -Commentary on politics and current issues 政治與時事評論 -Sport 體育新聞	-Human interest stories (of ordinary people in extraordinary situations) 富人性趣味的報導（有關於一般人非比平常的經歷） -Scandalous stories about the Royal family and celebrities 皇室與名人的醜聞 -Sport 體育新聞 -Gossip 八卦 -Pictures of pretty girls 清涼美女圖
新聞報導風格	-More factual and objective 事實客觀 -More formal, controlled, concise language 正式、收斂、準確的語言 -Difficult words and long sentences 艱深字眼及長句子 -Complex, interesting articles 複雜有趣的文章	-More sensational 較聳動 -Informal, short and very dramatic sentences 非正式、偏短的句子，非常戲劇性 -Lots of puns, quotes, jokes and exclamation marks (!) 很多雙關語、名言、笑話及驚嘆號！

各家報社除了每日發行的日報之外，也有週六及週日版。

The Saturday Guardian《週六衛報》厚厚一大疊，內容包括：News（新聞）、Sport（體育）、the Guardian Review（藝文評論）、Travel（旅遊）、Family（家庭關係）、Money（理財）、Work（求職）、Graduate（畢業生）、Weekend（週末）、The Guide（一週娛樂導覽）。*The Sunday Times*《泰晤士週日報》也是厚厚一大疊，內容包括：News（新聞）、Sport（體育）、Business（財經）、Comment（評論）、News Review（新聞評論）、Culture（藝文評論）、Style（時尚）、Travel（旅遊）、Driving（車訊）、Magazine（週日雜誌）。讀者一定很好奇，報紙內容這麼多，一天讀的完嗎？當然不可能。英國人看報的習慣是週六、週日看一部分，剩餘的留著接下來的一週慢慢讀。

讀者也可能會問：應該看哪一種報紙呢？從報紙版面來看，好像 Tabloids 的圖多字少，一目了然，似乎應該比較容易讀。事實恰好相反。英語是我們的第二語言，我們習慣讀合乎文法正式的英語，因此 Broadsheets 使用的正式英語，不涉及過多的特定英國社會文化背景，是比較適合我們閱讀的。Tabloids 的語言多用非正式英語（informal English）或俚語，可以拉近與讀者的距離。因此我們若是不了解文字的引申意義，就無法理解其中的幽默或諷刺。例如在報導犯罪事件時，Broadsheets 稱警察爲 police officer，Tabloids 則用 copper。又如警告一字，Tabloids 不用我們熟悉的 warn，卻用足球用語 yellow card（球員犯規時裁判出示警告的黃牌 yellow card）。我們都認識 warn 但 yellow card 則要有點足球知識才能理解。更麻煩的是，Tabloids 中的幽默、笑話及雙關語都與英國文化密切相關，需要具備部分文化認知（cultural literacy）才容易體會，因此，Tabloids 的內容對我們來說反而有些難以理解。

對英國報紙有了認識，讀者可以自行上網瀏覽免費的報紙網站，如 *The Guardian* (http://www.guardian.co.uk/)；*The Daily Telegraph* (http://www.telegraph.co.uk/)；*The Times* (http://www.thetimes.co.uk)。讀者會發現網路版的報紙，充分利用網路多媒體科技功能，有豐富的影像檔（videos）與聲音檔（audios），版面區塊色彩鮮明，吸引讀者閱讀。有的線上報紙是需要付費訂閱的，我會建議讀者只要閱讀免費的 *The*

Guardian 就已足夠。

至於紙本的報紙，我會推薦 *The Sunday Times*。該報內容豐富，英語也不困難。報紙不是英語課本，不需要全部都看懂（這是不可能的），更不需要遇到單字就查字典，不懂的字可以用猜的。報紙的內容五花八門，讀者只要撿自己有興趣的部分看看就好。能夠養成看一份週日或週六版報紙的習慣，你在英國的日子會非常忙碌充實，即有趣又可獲取新知。

為向讀者證明報紙內容不難懂，我從 *The Guardian* 及 *The Sunday Times* 選了幾部分，與讀者共享。

2.1a The Q & A 名人專訪

《衛報》的 Weekend「週末特刊」每期都有對名人專訪的 Q & A。我們看名人如何回答記者的問題，可以理解名人的內心世界與生活中的點點滴滴。下面的例子摘自不同名人的答案，有助於讀者學習一些常用字彙及句型，增加談話內容。

Q: When were you happiest?	**Q:** 你何時最快樂？
A1: On my wedding day.	**A1:** 結婚那天。
A2: At work, doing what I do best.	**A2:** 工作的時候，做我最擅長的事。
A3: When I was able finally to get out of bed when I had TB after two years.	**A3:** 得到肺結核時，病了兩年後，終於能夠下床的那一刻。

Q: What is your greatest fear?	**Q:** 你最害怕的事？
A1: Not have enough money to pay my tax bill.	**A1:** 錢不夠付所得稅。
A2: Losing the people I love.	**A2:** 失去我愛的人。
A3: Being locked in jail.	**A3:** 關在牢裡。

Dialogue 3 對話3

Q: What is your earliest memory?	**Q:** 最早的記憶是什麼？
A1: Being left in a big hall at primary school on my first day.	**A1:** 第一天上小學，被獨自留在大禮堂裡。
A2: Dancing around in my nappy.	**A2:** 包著尿布跳舞。

Dialogue 4 對話4

Q: Which living person do you most admire?	**Q:** 現今活著的人，你最仰慕誰？

A1: My nanny, my mum's mum.

A1: 我的外婆，我媽媽的媽媽。

A2: The Queen, for her loyalty and determination.

A2: 女王，因為她的忠誠與堅持。

Q: What is the trait you most deplore in yourself?

Q: 你最討厭自己哪一點？

A1: Getting distracted.

A1: 容易分心。

A2: I put myself under immense pressure.

A2: 給自己過大的壓力。

A3: Bad sense of time.

A3: 沒有時間觀念。

Q: What is the trait you most deplore in others?

Q: 你討厭的人有哪點特徵？

A1: Unkindness.

A1: 刻薄。

住所
平面媒體與通訊
日常生活
交通
休閒活動
醫療
BBC有趣的電視節目
閱讀廣告
附錄

A2: Prejudging people. → **A2:** 對人有成見。

A3: Bullying. → **A3:** 霸凌別人。

Dialogue 7 對話7

Q: Property aside, what's the most expensive thing you've bought? → **Q:** 不動產除外，你買過最貴的東西是什麼？

A1: Family holidays at Christmas. → **A1:** 聖誕節全家旅遊。

A2: Hiring a boat for the weekend. → **A2:** 租船度週末。

Dialogue 8 對話8

Q: What is your most treasured possession? → **Q:** 你最珍藏的財物是什麼？

A1: My photographs and Super 8 camera. → **A1:** 我的攝影作品及超 8 毫米攝影機。

A2: My voice. → **A2:** 我的聲音。

Dialogue 9 對話9

Q: What makes you unhappy?

Q: 何事讓你不樂？

A1: Losing things.

A1: 弄丟東西。

A2: The news.

A2: 新聞。

A3: Not being able to sing.

A3: 不能唱歌。

Q: What would your super power be?

Q: 你希望自己有什麼超能力？

A1: Time travel.

A1: 能夠穿越時空。

A2: Immortality.

A2: 長生不老。

Q: What is your most appalling habit?

Q: 你最糟糕的習慣是什麼？

A1: Interrupting.

A1: 打岔。

A2: Biting my nails.

A2: 咬指甲。

Dialogue 12 對話12

Q: Is it better to give or to receive?

Q: 施捨與收受哪樣好？

A1: You have to give to be able to receive.

A1: 你必須先付出才能收受。

A2: By giving you receive – it's a good deal.

A2: 付出就能收受——挺划得來。

Dialogue 13 對話13

Q: To whom would you most like to say sorry?

Q: 你最想對誰說抱歉？

A1: My mum and dad, because they're both dead now.

A1: 我父母，他們已不在世了。

A2: To my parents.

A2: 我的雙親。

Dialogue 14 對話14

Q: Which words or phrases do you most overuse?

Q: 你經常濫用的字或片語是什麼？

A1: Babe.

A1: 寶貝。

A2: Many swear words.

A2: 各種髒話。

Q: How do you relax?

Q: 你如何放鬆？

A1: Going to sleep.

A1: 去睡覺。

A2: I come home to my mum and dad's.

A2: 回父母家。

Q: What do you consider your greatest achievement?

Q: 你自認最大的成就是什麼？

A1: Still being married.

A1: 尚未離婚。

A2: Being knighted by Her Majesty.

A2: 被女王封爵。

Q: What keeps you awake at night?

Q: 什麼事讓你晚上睡不著？

A1: All those things I said out loud.

A1: 所有我大聲說過的話。

A2: Knowing I had to get up early.

A2: 想到要早起。

Q: How would you like to be remembered?

Q: 你希望別人怎麼記得你？

A1: She likes a laugh. And a cry. As a true and wonderful person, and a great actress.

A1: 她愛笑。也愛哭。一個真誠美好的人，也是一位偉大的女演員。

A2: As a singer.

A2: 是位歌手。

Q: What is the most important lesson life has taught you?

Q: 一生中最重要的教訓是什麼？

A1: Trying is the only way.

A1: 唯有不斷嘗試。

A2: To be strong, passionate, brave.

A2: 要堅強、熱情、勇敢。

A3: Don't make decisions when you've had too much to drink.

A3: 酒醉時不要做決定。

Dialogue20 對話20

Q: What is your guiltiest pleasure?

Q: 你最不好意思承認的享受是什麼？

A1: Horror films. I love being scared.

A1: 看恐怖片。我喜歡被嚇。

A2: White bread and salad cream.

A2: 白麵包和沙拉醬。

Q: Where would you like to live?

Q: 你想住在哪裡？

A: A place in London.

A: 倫敦某處。

Q: If you could go back in time, where would you go?

Q: 假如你可以回到過去，你想去哪個時間點？

A: Under the tree with Isaac Newton.

A: 和牛頓坐在樹下。

Q: What was your most embarrassing moment?

Q: 你最尷尬的時刻？

A: Being sick in the House of Lords on a school trip when I was nine.

A: 九歲時在參觀上議院的校外活動時，我在裡面嘔吐了。

Dialogue22 對話22

Q: What do you most dislike about your appearance?

Q: 對你的外表，最不喜歡哪一點？

A: My hands – I find them quite ungirly.

A: 我的手——不夠秀氣。

Q: What is your favourite word?

Q: 你最喜愛的字眼？

A: Hello!

A: 哈囉！

Q: What does love feel like?	**Q:**「愛」是什麼感覺？
A: Best feeling in the world, and worst.	**A:** 世上最美好也最壞的感覺。
Q: What has been your biggest disappointment?	**Q:** 人生最失意的事？
A: England losing in the World Cup.	**A:** 英格蘭國家隊輸掉世界盃足球賽。
Q: Have you ever said 'I love you' and not meant it?	**Q:** 你曾經口是心非地說「我愛你」嗎？
A: I always mean it.	**A:** 我向來是真心的。

2.1b Money 理財專欄

The Sunday Times《泰晤士週日報》有很多特別專欄，其中我最喜歡看的就是 Money 專刊中的「富豪理財」專訪。被訪問的對象都是當今富豪，讀這個專訪讓我們認識到很多富豪理財的概念，也發現原來他們都曾熬過苦日子。富豪們出入場合花費昂貴，因此他們每天需要帶很多現金。一般英國人平均每人身上帶的現鈔不會超過 50 英鎊，多半時候刷現金卡（Debit Card）消費。Debit Card 簽帳後，會直接從銀行戶頭扣款，等於是現金，與信用卡（Credit Card）不同。居住英國最好能申請一張 Debit

Card，不過 Credit Card 也是很好用的。

讀者可在這個專欄中，輕易地學到與理財相關的英語詞彙。

Q: How much money do you have in your wallet?

Q: 你皮夾裡有多少錢？

A1: About two hundred euros. I don't carry much cash nowadays.

A1: 大約 200 歐元。現在我不太帶現金出門。

A2: I don't really carry a wallet, but will sometimes put £20 or £50 in my back pocket.

A2: 我不帶皮夾，但有時會在褲子口袋裡放上 20 或 50 英鎊。

A3: I top up each day to make sure I have at least £200 before I leave the house. I like to tip in cash.

A3: 我每天出門前都會在皮夾裡補幾張鈔票，確保至少有 200 英鎊。我喜歡用現金給小費。

Q: What credit cards do you use?

Q: 你用哪幾家銀行的信用卡？

A1: I do most of my personal banking with Coutts and have the Coutts World Mastercard, which gives access to airport lounges.

A1: 我個人理財多半用 Coutts 銀行，他們發行的 Coutts World Mastercard 可讓我使用機場貴賓室。（註：Coutts 是英國老字號銀行，專門提供世界頂級富豪開戶理財的私人銀行。）

A2: I use the American Express Gold Card.

A2: 我用美國運通金卡。

Q: Are you a saver or a spender?

Q: 你是個節省的人還是個愛花錢的人？

A1: I am absolutely a saver. I don't like to spend money.

A1: 我絕對是以省錢為上。我不喜歡花錢。

A2: I'd describe myself as a profit maker.

A2: 我把自己定位為會賺錢的人。

A3: I am fortunate that I can afford to spend and to save.

A3: 我很幸運，即可以花也可以省。

Q: How much did you earn last year?

Q: 你去年賺了多少錢？

A1: Last time I looked, it came in at about £7m to £10m.

A1: 我最近查看的數字，大約是700萬到1000萬英鎊。

A2: I don't have a salary. I've got lots of businesses that are doing well.

A2: 我沒有薪水。不過很多生意的獲利都不錯。

Q: Have you really been hard up?

Q: 你曾經窮困過嗎？

A1: I earned just over £3 pounds a week when I was 17.

A1: 我 17 歲時，一週賺的錢只有 3 英鎊多一點。

A2: Yes, of course. I was in £250,000 credit card debt.

A2: 當然有窮過。我曾欠過卡債，約 25 萬英鎊。

A3: I remember most of my early life being difficult. I grew up in east London and my earliest memories are of cold, hunger and sickness. I started working when I was 14 and then I became an apprentice bricklayer. When I was 21, I opened a kiosk selling science fiction books and magazines near Charing Cross Station in London.

A3: 我記得早年的日子幾乎都很苦。我生長於倫敦東區，最早的記憶全與挨餓、受凍、生病有關。我 14 歲就開始工作，後來做砌磚學徒。21 歲時，我在倫敦 Charing Cross 車站附近開了一間專賣科幻小說與雜誌的書攤。

Q: Do you own a property?

Q: 你有房地產嗎？

A1: I have four. My main home is in Broughton Hall. I also have houses in west London.

A1: 我有 4 筆。我主要以 Broughton Hall 的房子為家，在倫敦西區也有幾棟房屋。

A2: I have homes in New York, San Francisco, Florida and South Africa.

A2: 我在紐約、舊金山、佛羅里達州和南非都有房子。

A3: I have a house in Surrey that I bought for £400,000 in 1993. I'd be disappointed if it wasn't valued at £7m today. It was built in 1850 and has seven bedrooms and 11 bathrooms. It sits on 55 acres of land.

A3: 我 1993 年在 Surrey 郡花了 40 萬英鎊買了一棟房子。今天它若沒有增值到 700 萬英鎊，我可是會很失望的。房子建於 1850 年，有 7 間臥室和 11 間浴室。連帶周圍的土地，面積有 55 英畝。

Q: Are you better off than your parents?

Q: 你比父母富裕嗎？

A1: Financially, of course.

A1: 經濟上，當然是的。

A2: Yes. My mother was a secretary.

A2: 是的。我母親以前是祕書。

A3: Yes. Before she got married, my mum was a bus conductor.

A3: 是的。我母親婚前是公車的車掌小姐。

Q: Do you invest in shares?

Q: 你投資股票嗎？

A1: I invest in a number of hedge funds.

A1: 我有投資幾個避險基金。

A2: Yes, I like to pick the companies in which I invest rather than rely on fund managers.

A2: 有，我喜歡自己挑選投資的公司，而不依賴基金經理人。

Q: What's better for retirement – property or pension?

Q: 退休哪一種投資較好？房地產還是退休基金？

A1: Property. Pension funds have suffered badly over the past four or five years.

A1: 房地產。退休基金最近 4、5 年受景氣影響縮得很嚴重。

A2: Shares, without a doubt.

A2: 毫無疑問股票較好。

A3: Personally, I rely on my business, but the pension and properties are a backstop.

A3: 就我個人而言，我寧可靠自己的生意，不過退休基金及房地產仍是種安全網。

Q: What's been your best investment in life?

Q: 你此生最好的投資是什麼？

A: Spending £20,000 on buying Ann Summers. It changed my life.

A: 花 2 萬英鎊買了 Ann Summers 公司，這改變了我的人生。（註：Ann Summers 公司於 2007-2008 年營業額已超過一億英鎊。）

Q: What has been your worst investment in life?

Q: 你此生最糟的投資是？

A: About 25 years ago, I lent money to someone I thought was a friend. As he was a friend, I just gave him the money－about £200,000 to buy a property to make a profit, and there was no paper work. When I went to visit, he had moved in and the whole thing was a scam. I asked him why he did it, and his response was simply that I was rich and he was poor. That was the end of our relationship.

A: 二十五年前，我借錢給一個我以為是朋友的人。因為這樣，我直接給了他 20 萬英鎊投資房地產，而沒有簽任何文件。後來我去看他，發現他自己住進買來投資的房子，整件事是場騙局。我問他為何那樣做，他只回答說，因為我有錢而他很窮。我們的友誼到此為止。

Dialogue12 對話12

Q: Do you manage your own financial affairs?

Q: 你自己理財嗎？

A1: Yes, although I use an accountant for the details.

A1: 是，但細節部分交給會計師處理。

A2: Mostly yes, though I have an accountant.

A2: 多半是，不過我有請會計師。

Q: What's the most extravagant thing you have ever bought?

Q: 你曾買過最奢侈的物品是什麼？

A1: I own a 72-metre superyacht.

A1: 我擁有一艘 72 米長的超級遊艇。

A2: Probably my New York property.

A2: 大概是我紐約的房產。

A3: I fly my own helicopter.

A3: 我駕駛自己的直升機。

Q: What's your money weakness?

Q: 你用錢的弱點是什麼？

A1: Giving money to charity. I've pledged to give at least half my wealth to charity.

A1: 捐錢給慈善機構。我已承諾將至少一半財富捐出去。

A2: I don't have one.

A2: 沒有。

A3: I like to splash out on expensive hotel rooms and eating out.

A3: 我愛花大錢住昂貴的酒店、上館子。

Dialogue 15 對話15

Q: What's your financial priority?

Q: 財務上你最看重哪一方面？

A1: To make a difference through my charitable work.

A1: 透過慈善工作改變世界。

A2: To help others to get financial freedom.

A2: 幫助別人得到經濟自由。

A3: To ensure my family and loved ones are taken care of.

A3: 確保我的家人及我愛的人受到照顧。

Dialogue 16 對話16

Q: What's the most important lesson you have learnt about money?

Q: 在金錢方面你學到最重要的教訓是什麼？

A1: A lack of it can create unhappiness.

A1: 沒有錢會造成不幸。

A2: While money alone will never make you happy, a lack of it will sure make you miserable.

A2: 只有金錢絕不會使你快樂，但沒有金錢肯定會很悲慘。

A3: Strive to make it and use it wisely.

A3: 努力賺錢，明智地使用。

Dialogue 17 對話17

Q: What would you do if you won the jackpot?	**Q:** 如果中了頭彩你想做什麼？
A: Give half to my football club and half to charity.	**A:** 一半給我的足球俱樂部，一半給慈善機構。

Dialogue 18 對話18

A: Do you do the lottery?	**A:** 你玩樂透嗎？
B: Yes, every week. I never miss it.	**B:** 是的，每週都買，從不缺席。
A: Have you ever won any-thing?	**A:** 有中獎嗎？
B: No, never. But I am sure I will one day.	**B:** 從來沒中過。我相信有一天會中。
A: What would you do if you won the lottery?	**A:** 中了樂透，你想做什麼。
B: I think I would buy a big house.	**B:** 我想買一棟大房子。

A: Would you give any money away?

A: 你會捐錢嗎？

B: Yes, of course, to a charity organisation.

B: 會的，捐給一個慈善機構。

A: How much money do you have in your wallet?

A: 你的錢包裡有多少錢？

B: A random assortment of dollars, pounds and euros. The tennis tour is global, so it's good to be prepared.

B: 有美金、英鎊、歐元。網球賽是全球性的，有備無患。

A: What credit cards do you use?

A: 你用哪一種信用卡？

B: I have a card with Adam & Company, a private bank. I always pay off my balance in full.

B: 我用一家私人銀行 Adam & Company 信用卡。我都付清帳單。

A: Are you a saver or a spender?

A: 你是節儉的人還是愛花錢的人？

B: Probably a saver, especially as a tennis career can be short. I try to invest as much as possible in things such as property. I've always been interested in property and it's something I'll continue being involved with after tennis.

B: 我是個節儉的人，因為網球生涯很短暫。我盡量投資如房地產。我對房地產很有興趣，網球結束後，也會繼續關注。

A: How much did you earn last year?

A: 你去年收入多少？

B: In total, about £8m. That includes £1.6m for winning Wimbledon.

B: 總共 800 萬英鎊。包括溫布頓的獎金 160 萬英鎊。

A: Have you ever been really hard up?

A: 你曾窮困過嗎？

B: When I left home at 15 to join the Sanchez-Casal Academy, the fees were high and I'm not sure how we were able to afford it as a family.

B: 我 15 歲離家進入 Sanchez-Casal 網球學院，它的費用很高，我也不確定我們家能否負擔得起。

A: Do you own a property?

A: 你有房產嗎？

B: My main residence has five bedrooms. I bought it new in 2009 for £5m. I also bought a couple of apartments in Miami, which I and my coach team use when I train over there.

B: 我經常居住的房子有五間臥室。2009 年用 500 萬英鎊買的。我在邁阿密買了幾間公寓，訓練期間，用來給教練團隊住。

A: Do you invest in property?

A: 你投資房地產嗎？

B: I've bought a luxury hotel in Scotland.

B: 我在蘇格蘭買了一棟豪華旅館。

A: What was your first job?

A: 你的第一份工作是什麼？

B: Playing tennis.

B: 打網球。

A: What's better for investment – property or pension?

A: 用來投資，房地產好還是退休基金？

B: You need both, but I do love property – it's simpler to understand.

B: 兩者都需要，我喜歡房地產，比較容易了解。

A: What's the most important lesson you have learnt about money?

A: 從金錢上你得到什麼教訓？

B: Not to take it for granted, so to respect it.

B: 不能將金錢視為當然，要尊重它。

2.1c Blind Date 相親專欄

The Saturday Guardian《週六衛報》包括好幾份副刊，其中 Weekend「週末特刊」特別爲想要交友的年輕男女設計一個 Blind Date（相親）專欄。被挑中的年輕人由報社安排到特選的餐廳會面。約會完畢，記者分別詢問兩人對彼此的印象。從記者的問題及答案中，我們可以了解到英國年輕人初次見面時，會注意對方的焦點，如談吐、衣著、餐桌禮儀等。英國人一般都很拘謹，重視個人隱私，不擅於跟陌生人交談，談話也不涉及個人隱私。因此第一次見面能輕鬆自在地侃侃而談，會被視爲是一種人格特質，也是優點。訪談結束後，記者會讓雙方就第一次見面的印象打個分數，通常以 10 分爲滿分。一般英國人看起來也許不是很友善，但一旦成爲朋友，卻可維持長久的友誼。

讀者會發現 Blind Date 專欄中的生活化英語是不難的。熟悉本專欄的問題及回答方式，有助於我們認識英國文化，同時學習如何回答問題，因此同一問題，提供不同答案供讀者參考。

Q: Before the date, what were you hoping for?

Q: 約會前你有何期待？

A1: Someone who can at least hold a conversation and is drop-dead gorgeous.

A1: 希望至少是個能談話和帥到不行的人。

A2: A good meal in decent company.

A2: 可跟不錯的人吃頓好飯。

Q: First impressions?

Q: 第一印象？

A1: Very smiley and relaxed.

A1: 很開朗自在。

A2: He was immaculately turned out.

A2: 他出現時，穿著得體。

Dialogue 3 對話3

Q: What did you talk about?

Q: 你們談些什麼？

A1: Our jobs, ambitions, travel. His love of Chinese history. All very intelligent and cultured.

A1: 我們的工作、志向、旅遊。他對中國歷史的興趣。內容全都非常知性、有文化。

A2: Mountains and rivers.

A2: 山野溪流。

A3: Student life, cooking, travelling, internet dating.

A3: 學生生活、烹飪、旅遊、線上交友。

Q: Any awkward moment?

Q: 有尷尬的片刻嗎？

A1: None.

A1: 沒有。

A2: We got to the tube together, he asked for my number but we reached his stop before I had time to give it.

A2: 我們一起搭地鐵，他向我要電話號碼，但我還沒來得及給，他就到站了。

Q: Good table manners?

Q: 飯桌禮儀好嗎？

A1: He was all elbows.

A1: 手肘一直放在桌子上。（註：吃飯手肘放在桌子上不禮貌。）

A2: Impeccable.

A2: 完美無瑕。

A3: Exemplary.

A3: 無可挑剔。

Q: Best thing about him?

Q: 他最好的地方？

A1: He is a very interesting chap.

A1: 他是個很有趣的人。

A2: Really easy to talk to; felt relaxed in his company.

A2: 很容易聊，跟他在一起很輕鬆。

Dialogue7 對話7

Q: Would you introduce him to your friends?

Q: 會介紹他給你的朋友認識嗎？

A1: They would enjoy a conversation with him as much as I did.

A1: 他們會跟我一樣覺得跟他聊天很愉快。

A2: He is very chatty, so I think so.

A2: 他很健談，所以應該會。

Q: Could he meet the parents?

Q: 能帶他去見爸媽嗎？

A1: As long as it wasn't over dinner. My mother has strict table manners.

A1: 不吃飯就行。我母親對餐桌禮儀很嚴格。

A2: He's got great manners and good chat, so probably.

A2: 他很有禮貌，善於交談，所以應該可以。

Q: Did you go on somewhere?

Q: 飯後有再去別的地方嗎？

A1: Our meal was three hours, so we called it a night.

A1: 這頓飯吃了 3 小時，所以就不再去哪裡了。

A2: No. It was a pleasant meal.

A2: 沒有。用餐很愉快。

A: If you could change one thing about this evening, what would it be?

A: 假如這次約會可以改變一件事，你希望改變什麼？

B: Nothing. I had a really nice evening.

B: 沒有。整晚都很愉快。

A: Would you meet again?

A: 你們會再見面嗎？

B: Happily, as friends.

B: 很樂意以朋友身分再見面。

A: Mark out of 10?

A: 10 分給幾分？

B: 7.

B: 7 分。

2.2 The Internet
網際網路

A: What's your email address?

A: 你的電子信箱？

B: wuhanwei@gmail.com

B: wuhanwei@gmail.com

A: Do you buy things on the internet?

A: 你會線上購物嗎？

B: Yes, I buy books.

B: 會，我買書。

A: What is the best web address for news?

A: 最好的新聞網站是哪一個？

B: I think BBC News (http://www.bbc.com/news/) is the best.

B: BBC News 是最好的新聞網站。

A: Which websites do you visit most?

A: 你最常瀏覽的網站是哪些？

B: Of course, BBC News.

B: 當然是 BBC 新聞網了。

A: Have you got broadband?

A: 你有寬頻嗎？

B: Yes, it's very fast.

B: 有的，速度很快。

A: How often do you go online?

A: 你多久上一次網？

B: I use the internet every evening.

B: 我每晚上網。

A: Do you visit chat rooms?
A: 你上網聊天嗎？

B: Yes, I often chat online.
B: 是的，我經常網上聊天。

A: Do you download music onto your computer?
A: 你會下載音樂到電腦上嗎？

B: Yes, or I download it onto my MP3 player.
B: 會，我也會下載到 MP3 上。

A: Which search engines do you use?
A: 你用那個搜尋引擎？

B: My favourite search engines are Google and Yahoo.
B: 我最喜愛的搜尋引擎是 Google 和 Yahoo。

Dialogue 2 對話2

A: Do you shop online in English?
A: 你常用英文網購嗎？

B: Yes, it is great, but sometimes I get problems.
B: 是的。很方便，但有問題。

A: What kind of problem?
A: 哪種問題？

B: The item I ordered is not always the right size. Sometimes the colour is wrong too.

B: 我訂購的物品尺寸不合。有時顏色也不對。

A: So what do you do?

A: 那怎麼辦？

B: Well, I have to put the item back in all the packaging. I go to the post office to send it back.

B: 我只好把物品再包起來。去郵局退回。

A: What a pain.

A: 真痛苦。

A: What do you do to stay safe on the internet?

A: 如何安全使用網路上網？

B: Never tell them where you live, where you go to school and where you work.

B: 永遠不要透露你的住處、學校及工作地點。

A: What is the easiest way to protect myself?

A: 最容易保護自己的方式是什麼？

B: We've all got passwords. So you've got to think about how you can get the best passwords.

B: 我們都有密碼。所以你要想個最好的密碼。

A: What should I avoid when I choose my passwords?

A: 選密碼要避免什麼？

B: Never use personal information. I recommend you use a combination of capital letters, small letters and numbers.

B: 絕不要用個人資訊。我建議你用大寫字母、小寫字母及數字的組合。

A: How do you feel about the Internet?

A: 你對網際網路的看法如何？

B: It makes my life easier. E-mail and instant messaging are useful for me at work.

B: 生活更方便。工作上電子郵件及簡訊對我很有用。

A: Do you use it at home?

A: 你在家也上網嗎？

B: When I am at home, I do a little online shopping, because it is so convenient.

B: 在家時我會上網購物，因為太方便了。

A: How do you feel about the Internet?

A: 你對網際網路有何看法？

B: The Internet is the best place to get the news. I am also taking this class because it is offered online. I have to use the Internet to do my homework.

B: 網路是獲取新聞最好的來源。我上這門課主要因為它是線上課程。我也上網做功課。

A: How do you feel about the Internet?

A: 你對網際網路有何看法？

B: I don't know how I'd live without it! I use it at work, as soon as I get home, I log on to my chat room to talk to my friends. I've just started my own blog!

B: 我無法想像沒有網路的日子。工作用網路，回家立刻登入聊天室與朋友聊天。我剛開了部落格。

2.3 Postal Service
郵寄業務

A: I would like to send this by priority post to Sweden.

A: 我要寄限時郵件到瑞典。

B: Can you put it on the scales, please?	**B:** 請放在磅秤上。
A: OK.	**A:** 好的。
B: Have you filled in a customs declaration form?	**B:** 你填申報單了嗎？
A: No, not yet.	**A:** 還沒有。
B: Please fill in this form. Contents, value, and your signature.	**B:** 請填寫這張表。註明內容、價值，並簽名。
A: How much will that be?	**A:** 多少錢？
B: £9.20. Anything else?	**B:** 9.20 英鎊。還需要別的嗎？
A: Yes, ten first-class stamps, ten second-class stamps, and ten European stamps.	**A:** 還要 10 張快捷郵票、10 張普通郵票、10 張歐洲郵票。
B: Here you are.	**B:** 都在這。
A: Thank you.	**A:** 謝謝。

Dialogue 2 對話2

A: Hello. I'd like to send this parcel to Germany, please.

A: 嗨，我要寄包裹到德國。

B: Put it on the scales, please. That's £5.20.

B: 請放在鎊秤上。共 5.20 英鎊。

A: Will it be there by Tuesday?

A: 週二會寄達嗎？

B: Well, it will if you send it special delivery but that's £4.20 extra.

B: 假如寄限時包裹就可以，不過要再加 4.20 英鎊。

A: OK then. And a book of first class stamps, please.

A: 好的。請再給我一本快捷郵票。

B: Certainly. That'll be £11.95 altogether.

B: 沒問題。一共是 11.95 英鎊。

2.4 Courier 快遞

A: Oh hello, it's Parcel Direct. I've got a parcel for you.

A: 嗨，這是 Parcel Direct 快遞。有你的包裹。

B: What is the name please?	**B:** 收件人的名字？
A: Mrs. Anne Smith.	**A:** 安妮・史密斯太太。
B: That's me.	**B:** 就是我。
A: Could you sign here please to confirm receipt?	**A:** 請在這簽名，確認收到。
B: Where do I sign?	**B:** 簽在哪？
A: Put your signature in the box. There you are.	**A:** 簽在方格中。好了。
B: Thank you very much.	**B:** 非常感謝。

Unit 3 Daily Life

日常生活

走到世界各地，日常生活接觸的事物，雖然大同小異，但文化差異使我們居住國外的生活充滿了挑戰。英國社會重要的禮儀之一就是 queuing（排隊）。讀者會發現在郵局、銀行、百貨公司結帳，都會看到 Queue here（在此排隊）的指標。不確定排隊方向，一定要問：'Excuse me, where is the queue?'（請問在哪排隊？）通常英國人是不會插隊的，但偶爾也會有人請求：'May I jump the queue?'（我可以插隊嗎？）而表達禮貌的字眼，如 Please, Sorry, Thank you 是英國人經常掛在嘴邊的。回答 yes 或 no 後面一定要加上 please，如 'Yes, please.' 'No, please.' 至於跟人打招呼，從天氣開始是最穩當的。本單元提供的英語對話、常用語句、提款機英語指令、公共場所的英語標示等，可幫助讀者應付日常生活所需要的英語能力。

3.1 Talking about the Weather 談天氣

A: Why are British people so interested in the weather?

A: 英國人為何對天氣如此有興趣？

B: British people talk about the weather all the time because it changes all the time. It gives us something to talk about. So if you run out of conversation, you can always talk about the weather.

B: 英國人永遠都愛談天氣，因為氣候變化多端。天氣是聊天題材。沒話說的時候，你就可以聊天氣。

A: Does the weather vary across the UK?

A: 英國天氣變化大嗎？

B: It can differ from one end of the country to another.

B: 從南到北都不一樣。

A: So what is the weather like for the rest of today?

A: 今天下半天的氣候如何？

B: It's not too bad across the United Kingdom. It is pretty nice for this summer.

B: 全國天氣都不錯。這樣的夏天很舒適。

1. 天氣如何？
What's the weather like?
2. 天氣預報如何？
What's the forecast?
3. 晴天 / 陰天 / 大風天 / 霧天 / 暴風雨 / 下冰雹 / 下雪天。
It is sunny / cloudy / windy / foggy / stormy / hailing / snowing.
4. 天氣真好！
What a nice day!
5. 真是美好的一天！
What a beautiful day!
6. 天氣不好。
It's not a very nice day.
7. 天氣真糟！
What a terrible day!
8. 要下雨了。
It's starting to rain.
9. 天氣很好。太陽出來了。萬里無雲。
The weather is fine. The sun has come out. There's not a cloud in the sky.
10. 太陽不見了。風很大。
The sun has just gone. There's a strong wind.
11. 又熱又潮溼。
It's hot and humid.
12. 像烤箱般的熱。
It's baking hot.
13. 天氣冰冷。
It's freezing cold.
14. 氣溫零下。
It's below zero.

15.聽起來像打雷。

That sounds like thunder.

16.那是閃電。

That's lightning.

17.我看到彩虹。

I can see the rainbow.

18.氣溫幾度？

What's the temperature?

19.昨夜有霜，車上有冰。

There was a frost last night; there's ice on the car.

20.我討厭這股熱浪。

I hate this heat wave.

21.下大雨我全身都溼透了。

It was pouring with rain and I got soaking wet.

22.攝氏 22 度。

It's 22°C (twenty-two degrees Centigrade).

23.潮溼的氣候令人不舒服。

Humid weather is very uncomfortable.

24.暴風雨時，你愛看閃電嗎？

Do you like watching lightning when it's stormy?

25.陣雨之間會出點太陽。

There was a bit of sunshine between the showers.

26.海邊會有涼風。

By the sea you get a nice breeze.

27.冬天晚間很冷。

In winter it's always freezing at night.

28.夏天通常熱又乾燥。

It's usually hot and dry in summer.

29.我們運氣不好，一連五天都是溼冷天。

We were out of luck: we had five cold, wet days in a row.

30.有足夠的雪可以滑雪，要好好利用。

There's plenty of snow for skiing, so let's make the most of it.

31.目前雨下的很大，但很快就會停。真是糟糕的天氣。

The rain is quite heavy at the moment, but it'll soon die out. What miserable weather we're having!

3.2a Weather Forecast 天氣預報

（本段取自英國報紙的天氣報導。讀者只要閱讀本段，熟悉英國地名及描述天氣的單字及句子，就可看懂電視氣象報導。）

Outlook 未來天氣預測

Mainly dry for England and Wales with variable cloud and sunny intervals, but fairly cloudy in the south-east for a time. Cloudy elsewhere with rain pushing into north-west Scotland as well as Northern Ireland later. 英格蘭及威爾斯無雨，多雲、時晴，東南方有時較多雲。其他地方多雲帶雨，先向蘇格蘭西北方移動，後移至北愛爾蘭。

UK Weather 英國各地天氣

Belfast 貝爾法斯特：Fairly cloudy 較多雲。

A largely cloudy day, but a few sunny intervals are possible.

陰天有可能偶有太陽。

Manchester 曼徹斯特：Sunny spells 偶晴。

It will be a dry and warmer day with spells of sunshine.

無雨暖和，偶有陽光。

Birmingham 伯明翰：Variable cloud 多雲。

It will be dry and fine with some sunny spells.

好天無雨偶晴。

Feeling warmer. 感覺較暖。

Cardiff 卡迪夫：Dry and fine 好天無雨。

A fair amount of cloud, but with some sunshine as well.

有些雲但也有些陽光。

Plymouth 普利茅斯：Sunny spells 偶晴。

Fairly cloudy at times but some sunny spells are possible.

偶多雲但也可能偶出太陽。

Portsmouth 朴茨茅斯：Fairly cloudy 較多雲。

It will be a generally cloudy day with just a few sunny intervals.
整天多雲僅有一陣陽光。
Edinburgh 愛丁堡：Largely cloudy 多雲。
A dry day, but it will be largely overcast. Feeling warmer.
無雨但陰天 感覺較暖。
Newcastle 紐卡索：Warmer 較暖。
A much warmer day, with sunny spells, but turning cloudier later.
非常暖和的一天，偶晴，稍後轉陰。
Leeds 利茲：Sunny spells 偶晴。
A dry and fine day with lengthy spells of sunshine developing.
好天無雨，形成長時間陽光。
Norwich 諾里奇：Sunshine later 稍後有陽光。
Largely cloudy for much of the morning, but brighter later.
清晨多雲，後有陽光。
London 倫敦：Clouds breaking 雲散開。
An overcast morning, but sunny spells should develop later.
早上陰天，後續偶出太陽。

想了解英國、與英國人溝通，首先要了解一般英國人經常談話的題材。也許讀者都知道英國人愛談天氣，爲何愛談天氣，值得說一說。

英國十八世紀文學家及詞典編撰大師約翰遜博士（Samuel Johnson, 1709-1784）曾說：「兩個英國人見面，第一件事就談天氣。」（When two Englishmen meet, their first talk is of the weather.）依據最新有關英國人習性的調查，有58%的人喜歡聊天氣，因此「談天氣」這個話題，依舊是榜首。到底天氣的魅力何在？原因有三：

(1)一般英國人見面談話小心，不會談論私事，以免因提問不當，引起雙方的尷尬。談論天氣，最安全，不涉及到個人的隱私。這是談天氣典型的情境對話語句：

Lovely day, isn't it? 天氣眞好，對吧。

What strange weather we are having. 眞是怪天氣。

It doesn't look like it's going to stop raining today. 今天的雨看來是不會停的。

(2)英國天氣從南到北，變化莫測，夏天也會下冰雹，一天四季，因此人人有話可說，都愛預測天氣。例如：

I think it'll clear up later. 我想稍後會放晴。

It's going to rain by the look of it. 看樣子會下雨。

They are expecting snow in the west. 西方有可能會下雪。

I hear that showers are coming our way. 我聽說大雨就要朝著我們來了。

(3)英國人喜愛園藝，天氣對植物的生長及花朵的顏色扮演重要因素，常見的景象是鄰居靠著花園的圍牆聊天氣。如果有人抱怨雨太多，種花的人會說：

Never mind, it's good for the garden. 別介意，雨對花園好。

對天氣太熱的反應：

At least my tomatoes will be happy. 至少番茄會很高興。

mild weather（溫和的氣候）、sunny spells（一陣陽光）、及 light drizzle（濛濛細雨）的天氣是園藝人士的最愛。對花園不利的氣候則是：a hard frost（霜凍）、blizzard（大風雪）、hailstones（冰雹）、prolonged rain（持續不斷的雨天）、a drought（乾旱）。

英國電視的氣象報導極爲詳盡，氣象播報員描寫天氣就像描寫一個有趣的人，講一個好聽的故事。報紙氣象預報欄出現有關天氣的英語字彙及語句都很固定。讀過本節提供的英國報紙中的氣象報導用語，熟悉這些語句，就可以欣賞電視的氣象報導，能恰當的用天氣做爲與人溝通的開場白。

interval	間隔
spell	一陣、短暫的
fairly	比一般多，但比很多少

variable	多變的
overcast	陰天、多雲
gale	暴風
heat wave	熱浪
high pressure	高氣壓
low pressure	低氣壓
weather forecast	天氣預報
global warning	全球暖化

3.2 At the Hairdresser's 上髮廊

A: I'd like to have my hair cut.

A: 我要剪頭髮。

B: How would you like me to cut it?

B: 你想剪什麼樣呢？

A: Not too short.

A: 不要剪太短。

A: Good morning, how can I help you?

A: 早安，有什麼可以為您服務的？

B: I'd like to make an appointment, please.

B: 我想約時間美髮。

A: What would you like to have done?

A: 您的需求是？

B: Well, I'm not sure so I would like to speak to a stylist.

B: 我還沒決定，所以我想跟造型師談談。

A: I can book you in for half past ten tomorrow morning. Please give me your name and number.

A: 明天上午 10:30 有空。請給我您的姓名與聯絡電話。

A: Hello, how can I help?

A: 哈囉，需要幫忙嗎？

B: Can I make an appointment, please?

B: 可以約時間嗎？

A: Yes, what would it be for?

A: 可以的，要做什麼服務？

B: Cut and colour.

B: 剪和染。

A: Let's have a look. We have a vacancy at three o'clock.

A: 讓我看一下。3點鐘有空。

B: Have you got anything earlier?

B: 可以早一點嗎？

A: Just let me check for you. Quarter past two?

A: 我再看看。2:15分如何？

B: Yes, that would be fine.

B: 那很好。

A: Have you had a colour with us before?

A: 你以前有在我們這裡染過頭髮嗎？

B: No, I haven't.

B: 沒有。

A: I will need to carry out a skin patch test to make sure you are not allergic to the colour.

A: 我需要做皮膚斑貼測試，確保你對染髮劑不會過敏。

B: That's fine.

B: 好的。

1. 我想留長，所以只要修一下。

   I'm letting it grow long, so just trim it, please.

2. 我要保留瀏海，往右旁分。

   I'd like to keep the fringe and the parting on the left.
   （Parting 指的是分線，故左右與中文用語不同。）

3. 跟原來的造型一樣。
   I want to keep the same hairstyle, please.
4. 多久需要剪一次頭髮？
   How often should I get my hair cut?
5. 我需要用洗髮精洗兩次嗎？
   Do I shampoo my hair twice when I wash it?
6. 這個潤絲精適合我的頭髮嗎？
   Am I using the right conditioner for my hair type?
7. 你有辦法幫忙改善我的髮質嗎？
   Is there anything you could do to improve the condition of my hair?

wash, cut and blow-dry	洗加剪加吹
permed	燙
straightened	燙直
colour	染
highlight	挑染

3.3 MOT Test 汽車檢修

A: When is my car eligible for its first MOT?

A: 我的車何時應該做 MOT 檢測？

B: When it is three years old.

B: 3 年就要做。

A: How long does an MOT test take?

A: 做 MOT 檢測需要多長時間？

B: Approximately 45 minutes, but it varies.

B: 大約 45 分鐘，情況不一。

A: Do I need to make an appointment for my car to be tested?

A: 在檢測汽車前需要預約嗎？

B: Normally, yes.

B: 通常需要的。

A: Am I notified when my test date is due?

A: 檢測時間到期，會通知我嗎？

B: Unlike road tax, where you receive a reminder, the MOT test is your responsibility.

B: 通行稅（或路稅）你會在到期前收到通知單，但 MOT 檢測則需自行負責。

A: My MOT is due on the 26/12/2016. Can I take it before that date?

A: 我的 MOT 2016 年 12 月 26 日到期。我可以提早做檢測嗎？

B: Yes, but the MOT certificate is only valid for 12 months from the date of the test.

B: 可以的，但是 MOT 證書的有效期限為 12 個月，是從檢測日期開始算。

A: Do I need to stay with my vehicle?

A: 我需要跟車嗎？

B: Normally no.

B: 通常不需要。

A: I have lost my MOT certificate, can I get a duplicate?

A: 若是遺失 MOT 證書，我可以拿到副本嗎？

B: Yes. The simplest way is to go back to the garage where the vehicle is tested. They should give you a duplicate certificate. You need to pay a fee.

B: 可以的。最簡單的方法就是到你車檢的修車廠。他們會給你證明書的副本。但要付費。
（註：英國開車每年需要付路稅（Road Tax），是一張圓的貼紙，有大字標明使用路權的期限。需貼在車窗上，交通警察很容易認出你的路稅有無過期。）

3.4 Form-filling 填表

在英國居住，辦理許多事情都需要填表格，如：申請工作、申辦信用卡、會員卡等。這類表格需要填寫的基本資料大同小異，英語也非常簡單，舉幾個例子，讀者一看就會。

範例一：填寫基本資料

First name 名
Surname 姓
Date of Birth 出生年月日
Title 稱呼 Mr. Mrs. Miss. Ms. 先生、太太、小姐、女士
Address 地址 Postcode 郵遞區號
Telephone 電話 Mobile phone 手機
Email 電子郵件
Which card are you applying for? 申請卡別
New Application 初次申請 Renewal 續卡
Adult 成人 Under 18 18 歲以下 Over 60 years 60 歲以上 Student 學生
Signed 簽名 Date 日期

範例二

這是訂閱雜誌時所需要填寫的表格，基本資料與範例一相同，但多了付款方式的部分。在英國訂閱雜誌普遍用 Direct Debit 自動扣款，由申請人向銀行要求從個人帳戶中撥款付給雜誌社。

Ms. / Miss. / Mrs. / Mr. 女士 / 小姐 / 太太 / 先生
First name 姓
Surname 名
Date of Birth 生日
Address 地址　　Postcode 郵遞區號
Home telephone number 住家電話號碼 Mobile telephone number 行動電話號碼
Email address 電子郵件地址
Please enter this information so that the *Hello Magazine UK* can keep you up to date with the latest offers, promotions and product information we think that you will enjoy. You can unsubscribe these magazines at any time. 請填寫此欄以便 *Hello Magazine UK* 幫你追蹤我們認為你會有興趣的最新優惠、促銷及產品訊息。任何時間都可取消訂閱。
Yes, I would like to subscribe to *Hello Magazine UK* for £15 12 issues by annual Direct Debit for a minimum of 12 months. 我願意付 15 英鎊，訂閱 12 期的 *Hello Magazine UK*，並同意以每年自動扣款方式，至少支付 12 個月的費用。
To the Manager (bank name) 致銀行經理（銀行名） Branch sort code 分行代碼 Bank account number 銀行帳號 Instruction to your Bank to pay Direct Debit. 授權銀行以自動扣款付款 Please pay *Hello Magazine UK* Direct Debit from the account detailed in this instruction, subject to the safeguards assured by the Direct Debit Guarantee. 請依據此指示，從該帳戶付款給 *Hello Magazine UK*。此授權已經受到「直接扣款保證」之保護。 Signature 簽名 Date 日期

範例三：求職表

應徵工作除填寫類似表格，並需提供過去雇主的資訊及推薦信。年齡滿16歲以上的年輕人，才可申請合法打工。

Position applied for: Temporary Christmas Jobs 應徵職位：聖誕節臨時工
Personal details 個人資料 Title: Mr. / Mrs. / Miss. / Ms. (please delete as applicable) 稱呼（刪去不合選項）
Surname: 姓 First name: 名 Name you like to be known as: 偏好的稱呼
Address: 地址 Postcode: 郵遞區號
Telephone (day): 電話（日）： (eve):（夜） mobile: 手機
Email: 電子郵件
Availability 可開始上班日
How many hours per week can you work? under 8 hrs 8-12 hrs 12-16 hrs 16-20 hrs 每週可工作時數？ 8 小時以下 8-12 小時 12-16 小時 16-20 小時
What are the maximum number of hours you could work in a week? 每週至多可工作幾小時？
Are there any days you cannot work? 每週有哪幾日無法上班？
Employment History 就業經歷 Employer's name and location 雇主姓名及工作地點 Job title and list of responsibilities 工作職稱及負責業務 Leaving salary and benefits 離職時薪資及津貼 Reason for leaving 離職原因
Why do you want to work for TK Maxx? 為何想在 TK Maxx 工作？

Additional information 附加資料

Please ensure you answer this section to the best of your knowledge.
請據實填寫本部分問題。

Do you require a work permit? 你需要工作許可嗎？

Do you have any criminal convictions? 你有前科嗎？

Do you require any special requirements to attend an interview?
你前來面試是否需要特殊安排？

If yes, please give details: 若有，請仔細說明。

Data Protection 資訊保護

We will use the information you have provided on this form and any information we obtain from third parties (such as people you have given as references) as part of the process assessing whether you are suitable for the job you have applied for.
我們會使用你在此表格內填寫的資料及從第三方（如你所提供的推薦人）取得的資訊，來評估你是否合適所申請的工作。

Declaration 聲明

I declare that I am 16 years of age or above and that, to the best of my knowledge, the information provided on this application is complete and correct. I understand that if I am offered the job, any false or misleading information would lead to withdrawal of this offer, or dismissal if I have commenced employment.
我謹聲明我年滿 16 歲，且本申請表上的資訊就我所知完整屬實。我了解我所提供的任何不正確或刻意誤導的資訊，將導致我失去聘用資格，或在已經被聘用的情況下遭到解聘。

I agree to the conditions of use. I confirm that the information I have provided is correct and I have no objections to the information being kept on a computer register. I understand that a photographic image will help prevent fraudulent use of the card.
我同意使用條件。我確認我所提供的資訊正確，也不反對此資訊保存在電腦紀錄中。我了解照片圖像有助於防止此卡遭到冒用。

Signed 簽名　　　　Date: (dd/mm/year) 日期（日/月/年）

If you do not wish to receive such information please tick here. 若你不想收到這些資訊，請在此打勾。

3.5 Signs in Public Places 公共場所標誌

1

Please do not swim or paddle in the lake or walk or skate on ice.
請勿在湖中划船或在冰上行走及溜冰。

2

Please don't feed bread to the waterfowl. 請勿用麵包餵食水鳥。

Feeding of bread can cause: poor nutrition, heart disease, over crowding, pollution, overdependence on humans, spread of disease.
餵食麵包會導致：營養不良、心臟疾病、過度擁擠、污染、過度依賴人類、散播疾病。

3

Dog Exercise Area 遛狗區
When using this area, it is the responsibility of the owners to ensure dogs are under control.
使用本區，主人有責任並確保管控好自己的狗狗。

4

Lake - Play Area - Maze 湖—遊樂區—迷宮
Dene - Bowling Greens 溪谷—草地保齡球
Saltwell Towers Saltwell 塔
Baby Changing 嬰兒盥洗室
Toilets 公廁

5

Gate 5 五號門

Saltwell Park is protected by CCTV Saltwell 公園裝有閉路電視監控

Gateshead Council Local Environment Services

Gateshead 市政府地方環保機構

24 hour Control Room　Telephone 0191 4775000

24 小時監控室　電話 0191 4775000

6

Free Car and Coach Park 免費汽車及大巴停車場
Footpath to the Park 往停車場步道
This car and coach park will be closed and locked at:
本汽車及大巴停車場關門及上鎖時間：
Local Environmental Services 24 hour Control Room Tel: 0191 4775000
本地環保機構 24 小時監控室　電話：0191 4775000
The council accepts no responsibility to loss or damage to vehicles parked in this car and coach park or contents thereof or personal injuries unless such loss, damage or personal injury is caused by the negligence of the council.
停在本停車場的汽車及大巴，若有財物遺失、損毀或當事人受傷，除非此過失歸咎市政府，否則市政府不負任何責任。

7

No stopping 禁止停車
Mon - Fri 週一—週五
8am - 5pm 上午 8 點—下午 5 點
on school entrance markings 校門口標示處

8

Symbols
Rail Station
Bus Station
Police Station
Visitor Information Points
Park & Ride Bus Stops
Park & Ride Site
Cathedral Bus Stops
Car Park
Coach Park
Public Toilet
Taxi Rank 10am-6am
Taxi Rank 8am-9pm
Taxi Rank 6pm-8am
Riverbank Walk avoiding steps

Rail Station 火車站　Bus Station 公車站　Police Station 警察局
Visitor Information Points 旅遊諮詢點
Park & Ride Bus Stops 停車場及公車站
Park & Ride Site 停車及搭車地點
Cathedral Bus Stops 大教堂公車站　Car Park 停車場
Coach Park 遊覽車停車場　Public Toilet 公廁
Taxi Rank 計程車招呼站
Riverbank Walk avoiding steps 無階梯河邊步道

9

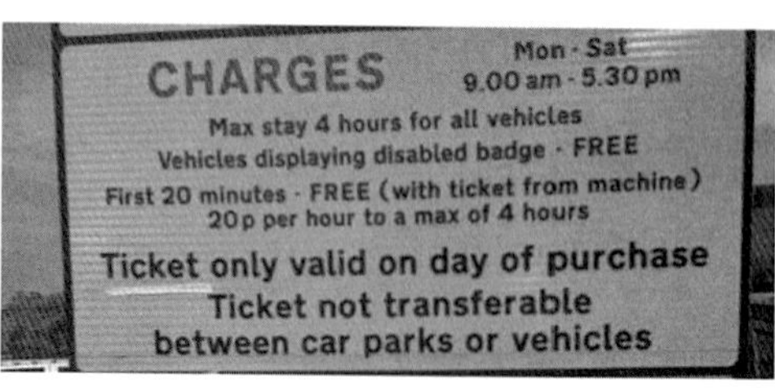

Charges 停車費
Max stay 4 hours for all vehicles 所有車輛不超過 4 小時
Vehicles displaying disabled badge - FREE 有殘疾人士停車證一免費
First 20 minutes - FREE (with ticket from machine)
前 20 分鐘免費（需有售票機的票）
20p per hour to a max of 4 hours 每小時 20p 不超過 4 小時

Ticket only valid on day of purchase 當日購票有效
Ticket not transferable between car parks or vehicles
停車票不可轉移用在其他車輛或停車場。

10

Have you paid and displayed ? 你有出示購票嗎？

11

Pay at machine 用購票機買票
Display ticket 出示停車票
Max stay 2 hours 最多停兩小時
To pay by phone call 02030032532 quoting location 13325
電話付費撥打 02030032532 地點代號 13325

12

Welcome to Haymarket Bus Station 歡迎來到 Haymarket 公車站

For the safety and comfort of all our passengers, please follow these rules.

為所有乘客的安全及舒適，請遵守下列規則。

No smoking 禁菸

It is against the law to smoke in this bus station.

在本公車站吸菸是違法的。

CCTV 閉路電視監控

CCTV cameras are in operation for the purpose of public safety, security and the detection of and prevention of crime.

設置閉路電視為公眾安全、防護、偵察及阻止犯罪。

This scheme is monitored by Newcastle City Council.

本計畫由 Newcastle 市政府監督。

For further information contact 0191 227 3437

更多資訊聯絡 0191 227 3437

Alcohol prohibited 禁止飲酒

It is against the law to consume alcohol in this station. Maximum fine on conviction is £500.

在本站飲酒是違法的。定罪最高可罰 500 英鎊。

Bicycles 腳踏車

Cycling is not allowed in this bus station. 本公車站禁騎腳踏車。

Skateboards 滑板

The use of skateboards and rollerblades is not allowed in this bus station. 本站禁用滑板及直排輪。

3.6 At the Bank
銀行

A: Can I use this card in this cash machine?

A: 這個提款機可以使用這張卡嗎？

B: If it's Visa Card, yes.

B: 萬事達卡是可以的。

A: Where can I change dollars into euros?

A: 我可以在哪裡將美金換成歐元？

B: In a bank, a hotel, or a bureau de change.

B: 在銀行、旅館、或外幣兌換店。

A: I want to make a withdrawal.

A: 我要提款。

B: How would you like the money?

B: 大鈔還是小鈔？

A: In tens, please.

A: 請給 10 英鎊紙鈔。

A: Is there a bureau de change near here?

A: 附近有外幣兌換店嗎？

B: Yes, there's one at the station.

B: 有的，在車站裡。

A: Where do I sign this?

A: 我在哪裡簽名？

B: Please sign on the dotted line.

B: 簽在虛線上。

A: What commission do you charge?

A: 手續費多少？

B: We charge 1%.

B: 我們收 1%。

A: I'd like to open a personal account.

A: 我想開戶。

B: Have you got any identification (ID)?

B: 你有證件嗎？

A: I've got my driving licence.

A: 我有駕照。

A: How do I open a UK bank account and what documents do I need?

A: 開英國銀行的戶頭需要什麼證件？

B: You will usually need documents to prove who you are and where you live. Example documents might be your passport and a utility bill with your name and UK address on it.

B: 你需要證件證明你的身分及住處。標準文件，如：你的護照及有你的名字和英國地址的水電費帳單。

A: What is an overdraft?

A: 透支是什麼？

B: An overdraft is when you withdraw more money that you actually have in your bank account. In many cases, unless you have overdraft protection, you can get fined for overdrawing on your account.

B: 透支就是你提的款超過你銀行的存款。除非你有透支保障，很多情況會罰款。

A: Could you tell me my balance, please?

A: 可以告訴我帳戶的結餘嗎？

B: Your account's overdrawn.

B: 你的帳戶透支了。

A: Could you transfer £1000 from my deposit account to my current account?

A: 請從我存款帳戶轉 1000 英鎊到我往來帳戶嗎？

A: How do I pay my TV Licence?

A: 我如何付電視執照費？

B: A standard TV Licence costs £145.50. There are three ways to pay. The easiest way is by annual Direct Debit because your TV Licence is automatically renewed every year. You can also spread the cost of your licence across four payments throughout the year. Monthly Direct Debit is our most popular option. You can pay for your twelve monthly instalments of just over £12.

B: 一般電視執照費是 145.50 英鎊一年。有三種付費方式：最簡單的方式是每年從帳戶中直接扣款，因為電視執照費每年自動更新。你也可以一年分四次付款。每月直接從戶頭扣款是常用的選項。分十二個月付款，每月只需 12 英鎊多一點。

1. 附近有提款機嗎？
Where is the nearest cash machine?

2. 可以給我小鈔嗎？
Could you give me some small notes?

3. 我要存這張支票。
I'd like to pay this cheque in, please.

4. 支票需要幾天兌現？
How many days will it take for the cheque to clear?

5. 我可以有一份帳單嗎？
Could I have a statement, please?

6. 我可以申請一本新的支票簿嗎？
Could I order a new cheque book, please?

7. 我要買外幣。
I'd like to order some foreign currency.

8. 歐元的匯率是多少？
What's the exchange rate for euros?

9. 我要取消這個定期支付的款項。
I'd like to cancel this standing order.

10. 這個帳戶的利率是多少？
What's the interest rate on this account?

11. 我想問一下有關貸款一事。
I'd like to speak to someone about a mortgage.

12. 目前個人貸款的利率是多少？
What's the current interest rate for personal loans?

13. 我要更換地址。
I'd like to tell you about a change of address.

14. 我可以約見一位理財專員嗎？
Could I make an appointment to see a financial advisor?

15. 我的銀行卡丟了。
I've lost my bank card.

16.我要申報被偷的信用卡。

I want to report a stolen credit card.

◆ **購物及使用提款機的英語指令**

Insert your card.	插卡。
confirm	確認密碼。
Withdraw cash.	提現鈔。
Your cash is being counted.	數鈔中。
Would you like a receipt?	需要收據？
Enter your pin.	輸入密碼。
Incorrect pin.	密碼錯誤。
Please wait.	請稍候。
Another service?	繼續服務？
Remove card.	取回卡。

Using your PIN 使用密碼

In order to help protect yourself against fraud, please do not use numbers that are easy to guess. 爲幫助防範詐騙，避免使用容易猜到的數字。

When changing your PIN you should avoid: 更改密碼時應避免：

1) your date of birth 你的生日
2) repeated numbers (1111) or (1234) 連續數字如 1111 或 1234
3) using the same PIN as another card 跟另一卡使用同一密碼

Best practice for keeping your PIN safe 保護密碼安全的最佳措施：

1) Never tell anyone your PIN. 勿將密碼告知他人。
2) Never write your PIN down. 不要將密碼寫下來。
3) Make sure no-one can see the PIN you enter when using your card. 確定使用銀行卡時無人看到你輸入的密碼。

註：Standing Order 客戶指示銀行定期轉帳支付的款項。英國人使用的 debit card（現金卡）密碼是四位數字。

3.7 Shopping 購物

民以食為天，走到世界各地，都需要解決民生問題。個人認為旅居英國，買菜購物需要與人口頭溝通的機會很少，但是能夠閱讀理解與食物相關的英語，比學一兩句對話更為實用。英國大型超市都設有熟食區、零售起司及魚肉專賣區。消費者可請店員依照個人需求挑選食物及重量。這種情境英語對話是很簡單的。讀者只需熟悉一些常用的英語句型，替換一些關鍵詞，就可達到溝通的目的了。

3.7a Shoppng at the supermarket 超市購物

A: I'd like some cheese, please.	**A:** 請 給 我 一 些 起司。
B: Sure. What would you like?	**B:** 好的。您要哪一種？

A: That Brie looks nice.	**A:** 這塊 Brie 看起來不錯。
B: Yes, it is. How much would you like?	**B:** 的確。您要多少？
A: About 250 grams.	**A:** 大約 250 克。
B: Right. This piece is just a little over.	**B:** 好的。這塊多了一點。
A: That's fine.	**A:** 沒關係。
B: Anything else?	**B:** 需要別的嗎？
A: No, that's it, thanks.	**A:** 不用了，這樣就好，謝謝。

Dialogue 2 對話2

A: Are you being served?	**A:** 能為您服務嗎？
B: I'd like six slices of ham.	**B:** 我要六片火腿肉。

Dialogue 3 對話3

A: That's £36.50.	**A:** 共 36.50 英鎊。
B: Could I have a carrier bag, please?	**B:** 可以給我一個塑膠袋嗎？
A: Do you need any help packing?	**A:** 需要幫忙打包嗎？
B: No, thanks.	**B:** 不用了，謝謝。

A: Would you like a baked apple pie?	**A:** 要烤蘋果派嗎？
B: Yes, please. They taste better than they look.	**B:** 要。吃起來比看起來好。

A: Bread and butter pudding?	**A:** 要麵包奶油布丁嗎？
B: Yes, please.	**B:** 要。

A: With cream?

A: 加奶油？

B: Yes, please.

B: 是的。

Dialogue6 對話6

A: Can I get the pasta bake, please?

A: 我可以來一份烤通心粉嗎？

B: You may indeed.

B: 當然可以。

Dialogue7 對話7

A: Would you like a drink?

A: 要喝飲料嗎？

B: Yes, please.

B: 是的。

A: Tea or coffee?

A: 茶還是咖啡？

B: Tea, please.

B: 茶。

A: Would you like milk and sugar?	**A:** 要加牛奶跟糖嗎？
B: Milk, no sugar. Thanks.	**B:** 牛奶就好，不用糖。謝謝。

Check out	結帳
10 items or less	十樣物品以下
Basket only	購物籃結帳
Cash only	現鈔結帳

3.7b Food labels 認識食品標示

英國是一個非常重視食品安全（Food Safety）及食品衛生（Food Hygiene）的國家。Food Standards Agency（食品標準機構）專門負責保護公民健康（public health）、規範食品工業（regulating food industry）及執行食品安全標準（enforcing food standards）。我們不需要深入了解英國嚴謹的食品法律，但能讀懂超市食品包裝盒的英語標示內容，是很實用的。

1. 食品標示保鮮期說明

   通常食品內容的說明包括三部分：(1) 食材或成分（Ingredients）；(2) 烹飪說明（Cooking Instructions）；(3) 儲藏（Storage）。所有食品皆須註明保存期：在此日期之前（Best before dates）、在此日期前食用（Use by dates）、出售日期（Sell by dates）、放在貨架至（Display until），以確保消費者不會買到過期的食品，對健康造成傷害。到底這些標示日期的文字有何不同？在此替讀者簡單做一說明。

Use by dates 指此類食物過期不可食用，儲藏不當會有害健康。包括：乳製品（Diary products）、鮮肉（Fresh meat）、魚（Fish）、家禽類（Poultry）、點心（Deserts）、沙拉（Salad）、熟食（Ready made meals）。

Best before dates 用來標示食品雖已到期，但只要品質良好，皆可食用。這類食品包括：冷凍食品（Frozen foods）、罐頭食品（Tinned foods）、餅乾（Biscuits）、飲料（Soft drinks）。至於 display until 及 sell by 主要是提醒超市員工要按時更換食品或補貨；而消費者則只需要注意 Use by 及 Best Before 的日期。

但此種標示日期的方法，往往會引起食品製造商及消費者對食物的浪費。英國相關部門曾就此問題做出澄清，日期的標示僅供消費者參考，並不表示食物品質會受到影響。因此消費者可以買超市打折的買一送一（Buy one get one free）即將到食用期限的熟食（Ready made meals），若不立刻食用，可冷藏，非常經濟划算。

2. 過敏食物警示

Food Standards Agency 規定超市食品必須用藍色標籤及文字警告對某些食物過敏人士，以免不小心誤食。其文字說明如下：

1) Allergy Information: containing Cow's Milk, Wheat, Gluten. 過敏資訊：包含牛奶、小麥、麩質。
2) Not suitable for NUT allergy sufferers due to manufacturing methods used. 因製作方法導致不適合果仁過敏人士食用。
3) No artificial colours or artificial flavourings. 無添加色素及香料。

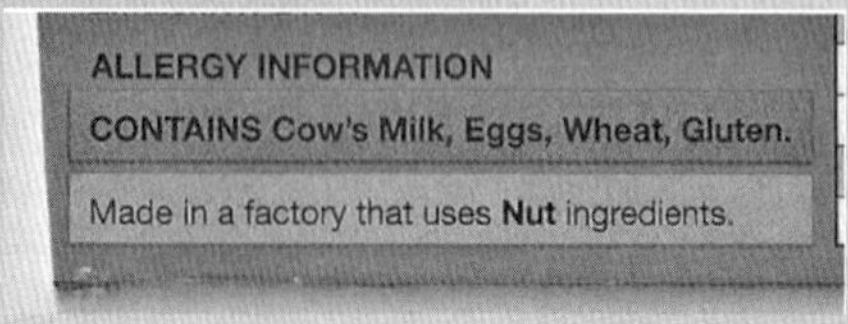

3. 消費者權益標示

爲顧及消費者的權益，若是買到不滿意或品質有問題的食品，食品包裝上也會註明可以退費。

1) We are sure you'll love this product. If you don't, simply return for a refund. 我們保證您會喜歡這個產品。若不喜歡，就可退貨退費。
2) We are committed to bringing you the best quality. Should you not be happy with the product, tell us and we'll replace it and refund you. 我們努力提供給您最好的品質。若您對產品不滿意，請告知，我們會替換並退費。

We're sure **you'll love this product.**
If you don't, simply return for a **full refund.**
Or call our careline **0800 636262.**
Your statutory rights are not affected.
Produced in the UK for
Sainsbury's Supermarkets Ltd,
London EC1N 2HT. www.sainsburys.co.uk
See reverse for storage instructions.

Unit 4 Transport

交通

網路科技帶給我們生活上重大的改變，透過電腦網路處理資訊，人與人需要開口說英語的機會減少了。旅居英國讀及聽的英語能力比口說能力來的更重要。入境英國，只需簡單回答移民官的問題，不會與他交談。搭乘飛機，若能聽懂機場及機艙內各種情況的英語廣播，可順利到達目的地。購買火車票需讀懂票上的資訊及乘車限制。聽懂火車站及倫敦地鐵的廣播，就不會搭錯車搞錯方向。認識英國公路指標可方便自駕出遊。這些都說明了，日常生活中，需要的英語能力是多方面的，而聽、讀的能力需求更高。本單元特別提供了機場、火車站、地鐵站的英語廣播文字資料，熟悉文字內容，有助於聽懂這些場合的廣播。

4.1 At the Airport
機場

假如有一種英語是全球英語（global English），世界各國的用法都是統一的、制式性的，那就是機場環境中出現的英語標誌、電腦螢幕顯示航班紀錄、告示牌、語音廣播。無論出國目的為何（長住、商務、留學、旅遊），只要踏出國門，乘坐飛機，面臨的就是英語。其實，機場環境中的英語並不難，只要熟悉一些固定的字彙及句子，便可應付出境、搭機、入境英國、回答移民官的制式問題、填寫入境表格。機場的情境對話，只有辦理登機時才有需要的幾句簡短英語。

A: I would like to check-in. I booked on the internet.	**A:** 我來辦登機。我在網路上預定的。
B: Do you have your booking reference?	**B:** 你有定位代號嗎？
A: Here's my booking reference, 8CP2SI.	**A:** 這是我的定位代號 8CP2SI。
B: Can I have your passport, please. Would you like a window or an aisle seat?	**B:** 請給我你的護照。請問要靠窗還是走道位子？
A: An aisle seat, please.	**A:** 走道的位子。
B: How many bags are you checking in?	**B:** 你有幾件托運行李？

A: One piece only.

A: 一件。

B: Could I see your hand luggage, please? Here is your boarding pass, Gate D56. Enjoy your flight!

B: 我可以看你的手提行李嗎？你的登機證，D56 登機門。祝旅途愉快！

- **Security 安檢**

1. 行李是自己打包的嗎？
   Did you pack your bags yourself?
2. 有人曾動過你的行李嗎？
   Has anyone had access to your bags?
3. 手提行李中有液體及尖銳物品嗎？
   Do you have any liquids or sharp objects in your hand luggage?
4. 請將外套脫下。
   Could you take off your coat, please?
5. 請將口袋中物品掏出。
   Please empty your pockets.
6. 請將金屬物品放在托盤中。
   Could you put any metallic objects into the tray, please?
7. 請將筆電從包包中取出。
   Please take your laptop out of its case.

In the Departure Lounge 候機室

1. 請問飛機班次？
   What's the flight number?
2. 是哪一個登機門？
   Which gate do we need?
3. 請立刻到 32 號登機門。
   Please proceed immediately to Gate number 32.
4. 航班延誤。
   The flight has been delayed.
5. 航班取消了。
   The flight has been cancelled.
6. 我們很抱歉班機延誤了。
   We would like to apologise for the delay.
7. 可以看一下護照及登機證嗎？
   Could I see your passport and boarding card, please?

On the Plane 機艙內常用英語

1. 請問你的座位是幾號？
   What's your seat number?
2. 請將個人的物品放在前面椅子的下面。
   Please place your personal items under the front of your seat.
3. 請關閉所有的手機及電子儀器。
   Please turn off all mobile phones and electronic devices.
4. 機長已將繫好安全帶指示燈打開／熄滅。
   The captain has switched on / switched off the Fasten Seatbelt sign.
5. 飛行時間需要多久？
   How long does the flight take?
6. 請問要用餐或點心嗎？
   Would you like any food or refreshments?
7. 十五分鐘後降落。
   We will be landing in about fifteen minutes.

8. 請繫好安全帶並回到座位上，將椅背豎直。

   Please fasten your seatbelt and return your seat to the upright position.

9. 請留在座位上直到飛機靜止以及繫好安帶的燈熄滅。

   Please stay in your seat until the aircraft has come to a complete standstill and the Fasten Seatbelt sign has been switched off.

10. 當地時間是晚上 9:34。

    The local time is 9:34 pm.

Airline Announcements 機場廣播

1. 飛往阿姆斯特丹的 KL 1048 班機已關閉。

   Flight KL 1048 to Amsterdam is now closed.

2. 這是飛往慕尼黑 BA 4021 班機最後廣播。請立刻前往 5 號登機門。

   This is the last call for passengers on flight BA 4021 to Munich. Please go to gate 5 immediately.

3. 飛往都柏林 FR 483 班機的旅客在 56 號機門登機。

   Passengers on flight FR 483 to Dublin: this flight is now boarding at gate 56.

4. 我們很抱歉飛往米蘭的 BA 7643 班機將延誤起飛。

   We are very sorry that BA 7643 to Milan is delayed.

5. 飛往米蘭的 BA 7643 班機即將於 11:50 起飛。

   Flight BA 7643 to Milan will now depart at 11:50.

6. 乘坐荷蘭航空公司第 1258 次航班前往曼徹斯特的旅客請到 B14 登機門。

   Passengers on Flight KLM 1258 to Manchester, please go to gate B14.

7. 這是荷蘭航空公司第 1258 次前往曼徹斯特航班的最後一次廣播，請立刻到 B14 登機門。

   This is the final call for passengers on Flight KLM 1258 to Manchester, please go urgently to gate B14.

8. 乘坐荷蘭航空公司第 1258 次航班前往曼徹斯特的旅客王大海先生，請立刻到 B14 登機門。你耽誤了航班起飛時間。

   Mr. Wang Da Ha on Flight KLM 1258 to Manchester, please go urgently to gate B14. You are delaying the flight.

9. 英國航空公司前往阿姆斯特丹第 471 次班機，現已在 C16 登機門開始登機。

   Flight BA471 to Amsterdam now boarding at gate C16.

Flight Timetable 航班時刻表

時間	航班編號	起飛地	狀態	航站
Sched.	Flight No.	Arriving from	Status	Terminal
14:50	AA6318	VENICE	SCHEDULED	5
14:50	AA6535	COPENHAGEN	SCHEDULED	5
14:50	AA6693	NEWCASTLE	CONTACT AIRLINE	5

時間	航班編號	目的地	狀態	航站
Sched.	Flight No.	Departing To	Status	Terminal
06:00	AC6156	VIENNA	SCHEDULED	1
06:00	BD2808	VIENNA	SCHEDULED	1
06:00	BD6785	ZURICH	SCHEDULED	1

Good afternoon, Ladies and Gentlemen. This is the pre-boarding announcement for flight BA471 to Rome. We are now inviting those passengers with small children, and any passengers requiring special assistance, to begin boarding at this time. Please have your boarding pass and identification ready. Regular boarding will begin in approximately ten minutes time. Thank you.

各位旅客午安。這是 BA471 到羅馬航班的預備登機廣播。我們先請有小孩的旅客、有需特別協助的旅客登機。請準備好您的登機證及護照，其他旅客約十分鐘後登機。謝謝。

Good morning, ladies and gentlemen. Welcome on board this British Airways flight to Rome. In a very short time, we'll be taking off. Our flight time today is two and a half hours, so we will be in Rome in time for lunch! The weather in Rome is clear and sunny, with a high of 28 degrees for this afternoon. The cabin crew will be serving refreshments during the flight, so just sit back and relax. We hope you will enjoy the flight. If you need any assistance, just press the button and a flight attendant will come to help you.

早安，女士們、先生們。歡迎搭乘英航飛往羅馬的班機。我們很快就要起飛了。今日飛行時間為兩小時又三十分鐘，所以我們可以趕上在羅馬吃中餐。羅馬天氣晴朗，氣溫攝氏 28 度。空服員即將供應餐點，放輕鬆休息。我們祝您飛行愉快。若需要協助，只要按鈴，空服員會前來幫忙。

In twenty minutes' time we will be landing. Please put your seats into the upright position. Make sure your seatbelt is securely fastened and all your hand luggage is stowed underneath the seat in front of you. Please remain seated until the plane has come to a complete standstill. Before you leave the plane, please take all your personal belongings with you.

二十分鐘後我們即將降落。請將椅背豎好。請繫好安全帶並將隨身物品放在前面的座椅下。在飛機完全停止前，請不要離開座位。下機時請不要忘了隨身攜帶的行李。

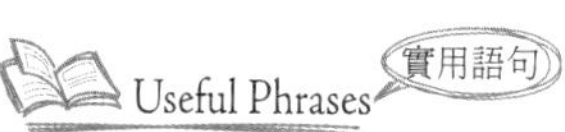

1. 請出示你的護照。
   Could I see your passport, please?
2. 你從哪裡來？
   Where have you travelled from?
3. 為何來此地？
   What's the purpose of your visit?
4. 我來度假／洽商／探親。
   I'm on holiday / on business / visiting relatives.
5. 你停留多久？
   How long will you be staying?
6. 住在何處？
   Where will you be staying?
7. 請填好入境卡。
   You have to fill in this landing card.
8. 請打開你的手提包。
   Could you open your bag, please?
9. 有要申報的物品嗎？
   Do you have anything to declare?

10.這幾樣物品要繳關稅。

You have to pay duty on these items.

◆ 在機場中你會經常看到的英語標誌

Online Check-in Boarding Pass	網上預辦登機證
Flight connections	銜接航班
Nothing to declare	無申報
International flights	國際航班
Delayed	延誤
Cancelled	取消
Boarding sequence	登機順序
Gate closed	登機門已關閉
Expected	預計到達
scheduled	準時
Transfers	轉機
Tax free shopping	免稅商店
Good to declare	申報
Domestic flights	國內航班
Now boarding	登機中
Last call	最後一次廣播
Departed	已飛
Landed	已到

◆ 證照檢查處標示

Home Office	內政部
UK Border Agency	英國國境局
EU citizens	歐盟人士
All passports	其他國籍
Wait behind the yellow line.	在黃線後等待。
Please have your passport ready.	請將護照準備好。

Notes 小叮嚀

◆ Landing Card 入境卡

入境英國需要填寫一張 Landing Card 入境卡。在此將入境卡的英語譯成中文，讓讀者了解需要填寫的資料。

Please complete clearly in English and BLOCK CAPITALS.
請以英文大寫字母清楚填寫。

Family name……………………………………姓
First name(s)…………………………………名
Sex M F 性別 Date of Birth DDMMYYYY 出生日月年

Town and Country of birth…………………………出生地
Nationality……………國籍 Occupation……………職業
Contact address in the UK (in full) 英國詳細住址
…………………………………………………………………………………
Passport no. ………護照號碼 Place of issue……發照地
Length of stay in the UK ……………停留時間
Port of last departure ……………來自何地
Arrival flight / train number / ship name 入境班機 / 火車班次 / 船名
Signature ……………………………………………………簽名

IF YOU BREAK UK LAWS YOU COULD FACE IMPRISONMENT AND REMOVAL. 你若觸犯英國法律，可能面臨監禁或遭遞解出境。

小提示：英式英語填寫日期的順序是：日、月、年。

4.2 British Rail
英國火車

英國的大眾交通工具如火車、公車、地鐵的票價是相當昂貴的。火車票價的高低與火車時段、有無轉乘（change）、行車時間長短相關。高價位的全額票與優惠票差價很大。可以買到便宜的折扣票（cheap fares），數量有限，不但要及早購買（通常是三個月就可開買），也有許多乘車的條件與限制（Terms and Conditions）。鐵路公司網站會清楚告知乘客購買優惠票的方法。

A: I'd like two tickets, please.	**A:** 買兩張票。
B: Where to?	**B:** 到哪裡？
A: One to Oxford and the other to Cambridge.	**A:** 一張到牛津，一張到劍橋。
B: Single or return?	**B:** 單程還是來回票？
A: Single, please.	**A:** 單程票。
B: That's £40.50.	**B:** 共 40.50 英鎊。

A: Thanks. | A: 謝謝。

A: A ticket to Oxford, please. | A: 買一張去牛津的票。

B: Single or return? | B: 單程還是來回票？

A: Return. | A: 來回票。

B: Thirty pounds twenty. | B: 30 英鎊 20 便士。

A: OK. | A: 好的。

Dialogue 3 對話3

A: Excuse me. Do you know what time the next train to London leaves? | A: 請問下班開往倫敦的火車是幾點？

B: There's one at 5 o'clock. | B: 五點鐘有一班。

A: What's the time? Oh, no. I have missed that one.

A: 現在幾點？糟了，我錯過那班車了。

B: There's another one at 6:45. You'd better hurry.

B: 6:45 還有一班，你得趕快。

A: A single to Cardiff, please.

A: 一張去 Cardiff 的單程票。

B: That's £14.80, please.

B: 14.80 英鎊。

A: Right, and when's the next train?

A: 好的，下班車是幾點？

B: There's one at 10:21.

B: 10:21 有一班。

A: Fine. Do I have to change?

A: 好的。需要換車嗎？

B: No, it's direct.

B: 不需要，是直達車。

A: That's good. And when does it get to Cardiff?

A: 很好。幾點到 Cardiff？

B: 11:23.	**B:** 11:23。
A: OK. And which platform is it?	**A:** 好，哪個月臺？
B: Platform 6.	**B:** 第 6 月臺。
A: Right, thanks.	**A:** 很好。謝謝。（註：英國人多用 Right，雖然用 OK 也很普遍。）

1. 售票處在哪裡？
   Where's the ticket office?
2. 哪裡有售票機？
   Where are the ticket machines?
3. 下一班去愛丁堡的火車是幾點鐘？
   What time's the next train to Edinburgh?
4. 我可以在火車上買票嗎？
   Can I buy a ticket on the train?
5. 到倫敦的單程票／來回票／頭等單程票／頭等來回票多少錢？
   How much is a single / a return / a first class single / a first class return to London?
6. 有離峰時間出行的減價票嗎？
   Are there any reductions for off-peak travel?
7. 你想何時出行？
   When would you like to travel?

8. 買一張去約克的來回票，回程是星期天。

I'd like a return to York, coming back on Sunday.

9. 去曼徹斯特的月臺是哪一號？

Which platform do I need for Manchester?

10. 這是去倫敦尤斯頓站的月臺，對吧？

Is this the right platform for London Euston?

11. 去約克在哪裡換車？

Where do I change for York?

12. 你需在愛丁堡換車。

You'll need to change at Edinburgh.

13. 可以給我一份時刻表嗎？

Can I have a timetable, please?

14. 去卡迪夫的火車多久一班？

How often do the trains run to Cardiff?

15. 請出示車票。

Tickets, please.

16. 我的車票不見了。

I've lost my ticket.

17. 我們幾點到牛津？

What time do we arrive in Oxford?

18. 這是哪一站？

What's this stop?

19. 下一站是哪裡？

What's the next stop?

20. 火車誤點了。

The train's running late.

21. 火車取消了。

The train's been cancelled.

22. 這班火車會在杜倫停嗎？

Does this train stop at Durham?

23. 這位子有人坐嗎？

Is this seat taken?

24.我可以坐這個位子嗎？

Do you mind if I sit here?

25.我可以開窗嗎？

Do you mind if I open the window?

26.我想坐 8:30 的車，可是我的回程票限定我只能坐 9:30 以後的班次。

I wanted to leave at 8:30, but my day return was only valid after 9:30.

27.火車應該 9:42 到，但到 11:40 才進站。

The train was due at 9:42 but it didn't get in until 11:40.

28.我遲到了，因為火車班次無預警的取消了。

I was late because they cancelled my train without warning.

◆ **Signs in Train Station 火車站的英語標示**

Tickets	購票處
Platform	月臺
Waiting room	候車室
Left luggage	寄存行李
Lost property	失物招領
Underground	地鐵
On time	準時
Expected	預定到達時間
Delayed	延誤
Cancelled	取消
Priority seat	博愛座

◆ **Train Announcement 火車廣播**

The next train to arrive at Platform 2 is the 16:35 to Doncaster.

下一班到達二號月臺的列車，是 16:35 開往東克斯特。

The next train to depart from Platform 5 will be the 18:03 service to Newcastle.

下一班即將離開第五月臺的火車是 18:03 開往紐卡索。

We will be calling at Durham, Leeds, Sheffield, Luton and London.

本次列車停靠杜倫、利茲、謝菲爾德、魯頓、倫敦。

Please mind the gap between the train and the platform edge.

注意車廂與月臺的空隙。

We are now approaching London Euston.

我們即將到達倫敦尤斯頓站。

This train terminates here.

這是本列車的終點站。

If you leave the train, please make sure to take all your personal belongings with you.

下車時，請務必將您個人的物品帶走。

維珍鐵路（Virgin Trains）的網站（http://www.virgintrains.co.uk/tickets-offers/）列出購票省錢三步驟：

(1) Think ahead: The further in advance you book, the more you save (up to 3 months). 及早計畫：愈早（三個月）預定票省越多。

(2) Travel off-peak: Travel off-peak to find a cheaper ticket. 避開尖峰時段，可找到最便宜的票。

(3) Be flexible: Be flexible with dates and times. 日期與時間最好有彈性。

把握這三個原則，應該可以買到優惠的火車票，但要注意車票的限制，以免遭罰。另外，有時買兩張單程去回的火車票比一張來回票便宜，有時一張來回票比一張單程票還便宜。所以說，在英國過日子，凡事需要及早計畫安排日程，臨時購票沒有選擇，只能買昂貴的全額票，心理會很不平衡的。

這是一張火車票所包括的信息：

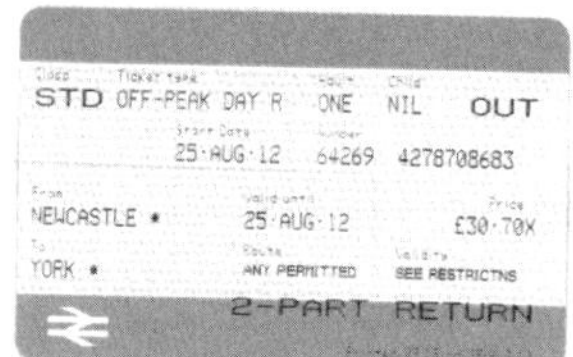

Train Ticket

Class 等級　Ticket Type 票類　Adult 成人　Child 兒童

Out / RTN 去 / 回

STD 普通座　Off-Peak Day 非尖峰日　One　Nil 無

Start Date 日期　Number 編號

25 August 12　64269 4278708683

From 起點　Valid until 有效期限　Price 票價

Newcastle　25 August 12　£30.70

To 到達地　Route 路線　Validity 有效性

York　Any Permitted 任何路線皆可　See Restrictions 見限制條件

4.3 Motorway 高速公路

在英國開車跟日本一樣，都是左邊開車（drive on the left），駕駛座在右邊。倫敦斑馬線路面寫著大字 look left 提醒行人注意看左邊來車。英國高速公路限速 70 miles（可能會提速到 80 miles），三線道。道路用字母加上阿拉伯數字來標示：M 代表 Motorway（高速公路），其他有 A Road 及 B Road 開車最重要的是方向要對，也要找到正確的 junction 交流道。

Dialogue 1 對話1

A: How far is it from London to Bath?

A: 從倫敦到巴斯有多遠？

B: It's about 100 miles. It usually takes between one hour 40 minutes to two hours.

B: 100 多英里。通常需要 1 小時 40 分到兩小時。

A: What is the best way to get there?

A: 怎麼去最方便？

B: Take the M4 motorway from London. At junction 18 turn off and turn left onto the A46 to Bath. It's 8 miles from there. You will drive through a couple of roundabouts – always follow the signs to Bath.

B: 從倫敦上 M4 高速公路。18 號交流道下來左轉到 A46 就到 Bath 了。從這裡到巴斯只有 8 英里。你會經過幾個環狀道一照著巴斯的指標開就到了。

A: Thanks. And what's the speed limit on motorways here?

A: 謝謝。這裡高速公路的限速是多少？

B: 70 miles an hour.

B: 時速 70 英里。

A: Are the motorways very busy?

A: 高速公路車多嗎？

B: Yes, and you get traffic jams in the rush hour.

B: 是的。尖峰時段會塞車。

A: But you still use the motorway?

A: 但還是要走高速公路？

B: Yes, there are three lanes on most motorways in Britain.

B: 是的，英國高速公路是三線道。

Dialogue 2 對話2

A: When did you first learn to drive?

A: 你何時開始學開車？

B: I didn't start learning to drive until I was 30.

B: 我到 30 歲才開始。

A: When did you get your driving licence?

A: 你何時考到駕照？

B: I got it when I was 35.

B: 我 35 歲考上。

A: Do you like driving?

A: 你喜歡開車嗎？

B: No, I don't. I prefer cycling.

B: 不喜歡。我愛騎腳踏車。

A: What car have you got now?

A: 你現在開什麼車？

B: I've got a Nissan Micra.

B: 開 Nissan Micra。

A: What's your dream car?

A: 你夢想的車？

B: An Aston Martin DB11, of course.

B: 當然是超級跑車 Aston Martin DB11 囉。

A: What do you hate most about other drivers?

A: 你最討厭哪一類駕駛人？

B: When they drive right behind me on the motorway.

B: 高速公路上緊跟在我後面人。

A: Do you usually brake and accelerate gently?

A: 你通常煞車及加速都很輕嗎？

B: Usually I do, but I accelerate quickly to overtake.

B: 通常是這樣的，但超車時要加速。

A: Do you usually reverse into parking spaces in a car park?

A: 你通常都倒車入庫嗎？

B: No, not always.	**B:** 不常。
A: Are there times when you don't keep to the speed limit?	**A:** 你有超速的時候吧？
B: Yes, usually on motorways.	**B:** 有的，通常在高速公路上。
A: Do you know what to do if your car skids?	**A:** 你知道開車打滑要怎麼辦？
B: I know what to do but sometimes I panic and forget.	**B:** 我知道要怎麼做，但有時慌起來都忘了。

Top Tips for New Drivers 新手上路重要提示

1. Slow down. Many new drivers go too fast. Remember, if you're driving slower you stand a better chance of avoiding an accident if anything unexpected happens. 開車要慢。大多新手都開太快。記住，有任何意外發生，開的慢有較好的機會可以避免事故。
2. Remember to check your seat belt, mirror, etc. before you pullout from the side of the road into traffic. 在上路前，記住檢查安全帶、後照鏡等。
3. Don't drive if you're feeling sleepy. If necessary, break your journey and have a coffee. 如果你想睡覺時別開車。可能的話，最好將旅程分段開，喝杯咖啡提神。
4. Be prepared for anything on long journeys if you're alone. Make sure you fill the car up with petrol, and take a

mobile phone with you, just in case you break down in the middle of nowhere. 獨自長途開車，要做好準備。加滿油、帶好手機、以防在荒郊出故障。

5.Also, on long journeys, check the oil and tyre pressure before you set off. 長途旅程，出發前要檢查油及輪胎氣壓。

6.If your mobile rings, don't answer it. Wait until it is safe to pull to the side of the road and then answer the call. 如果手機響了，別接。將車安全開到路邊，再接。

Tips for safer driving 安全駕駛提示

1.Always be prepared for bad road conditions and bad drivers. 對不良路況及不良駕駛人做好防範。

2.On wet roads, brake, steer, and accelerate gently to avoid skidding. 在溼滑的路面上，煞車、打方向盤、加速都要輕，以免打滑。

3.Watch out for motorcyclists and cyclists; give them plenty of space when overtaking. 注意騎摩托車及腳踏車的人，超車時要保持夠距離。

4.In car parks, reverse into a parking space. 在停車場，最好倒車入位。

5.Keep to the speed limit and don't drive too close to the vehicle in front. 不要超速也不要距前車太近。

Traffic Signs 交通標誌

1 T 符號代表此路不通。

2 Roundabouts 環狀繞行路標

這是一個典型的 Roundabout 標示。在英國開車經常會看到這個標誌。綠色 A1 是道路編號，Motorway 高速公路是藍色。

行駛方式：(1) 進入環線左邊 Town Centre 叫 the first exit（第一出口），打左轉方向燈靠左行駛。(2) 中間 Low Fell 叫 the second exit（第二出口），先打右轉方向燈靠右行駛，過了 the first exit 時，立刻打左轉燈靠左出口。(3) 右邊 Harlow Green /Wrekenton 叫 the third exit（第三出口），先打右轉燈靠右行駛，過了 the second exit 時，立刻打左轉燈靠左行駛出口。這是英國駕照路考必考的項目。方向燈打錯就要重考。

3 Bus Timetable 公車班次時間表

公車站牌提供的公車行駛時間表通常會準時到站。行車時間會依季節調整，故需注意生效日期（effect from）。讀者會發現公車行駛時間上班日班次密集，週六、日班次較少。typical journey times 是指每一站的行車時間；then at 06, 21, 36, 51 mins past each hour until 指之後每小時 6 分、21 分、36 分、51 分直到下列班次。

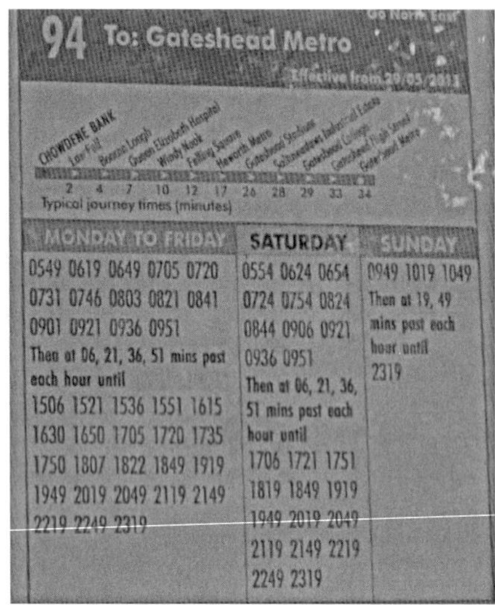

4.4 The London Underground 倫敦地鐵

倫敦重要的大衆交通工具是 The Underground（地鐵），非正式英語稱 The Tube，乘坐倫敦地鐵使用 Oyster Card（牡蠣卡，類似我們的悠遊卡）或 Travelcard（旅遊卡）。票價按照劃分的 Zones（區）核算。地鐵每一條線都有名稱並用不同顏色標示。讀者乘坐地鐵會看到月臺方向指標，如 Westbound Platform（往西方向月臺）、Southbound Platform（往南方向月臺）、Northbound Platform（往北方向月臺）、Eastbound Platform（往東方向月臺），以免乘錯方向。乘坐地鐵也要注意聽廣播。這類英語表達方式多半是制式性的，了解句子結構，熟悉英文名稱，就能把握搭乘地鐵要領。

A: I'd like an Oyster card, please.

A: 買一張牡蠣乘車卡。

B: Which zones?

B: 哪個區？

A: Zones 1-2.

A: 1-2 區。

A: Could you tell me where the nearest Tube station is?

A: 請問最近的地鐵站在哪裡？

B: Walk two blocks and turn left.

B: 走兩條街左轉。

A: Which line do I need for Covent Garden?

A: 到 Covent Garden 應坐哪一條線？

B: You need the Piccadilly Line.

B: 坐 Piccadilly 線。

A: We take the blue line?

A: 我們坐藍線，對吧？

B: Yes, it's called the Piccadilly Line, but which direction?

B: 是的，是 Piccadilly 線，可是往哪個方向？

A: We're at the end of the line so we go eastbound.

A: 這是本線的終點，所以要往東。

B: Do we have to change trains?

B: 我們要換車嗎？

A: Mine's direct, but you have to get off and change.

A: 我的車直達，你要下車換乘。

B: But I can change at King's Cross, so we can both get off together.

B: 我可以在 King's Cross 換車，這樣我們可以一起下車。

A: And then you take this black line, the Northern Line, and go north.

A: 你可以換乘黑線，往北的 Northern 線。

Dialogue4 對話4

A: Should I get a London Travelcard or Oyster Card?

A: 我要買旅遊卡還是牡蠣卡？

B: It depends how long you are staying in London and how frequently you'll be using public transport.

B: 這要看你在倫敦的時間以及你乘大眾交通次數。

A: Are there any time restrictions when using the Oyster Card?

A: 使用牡蠣卡有時間限制嗎？

B: Your Oyster Card can be used at any time. Peak times are more expensive.

B: 牡蠣卡任何時間都可以用，但尖峰時間較貴。

A: Can I buy an Oyster Card online?

A: 我能在網上買牡蠣卡嗎？

B: You can buy your card from the VisitBritain Shop and it will be mailed to you at your home address.

B: 你可以在 VisitBritain Shop 網店購買，會寄到你家的地址。

A: Can I use my Oyster Card to get the Tube from Heathrow to London or from London to Heathrow?

A: 我可以用牡蠣卡乘坐 Heathrow 機場到倫敦來回的地鐵嗎？

B: Yes, Heathrow Airport is on the Piccadilly Line in London travel zone 6.

B: 可以的。機場是 Piccadilly 線的第六區。

A: How long does the Tube take from Heathrow to London ?

A: 從機場到倫敦坐地鐵要多久？

B: The journey time between Heathrow Airport and central London is around 50 minutes.

B: 搭地鐵從機場到倫敦市中心大約要 50 分鐘。

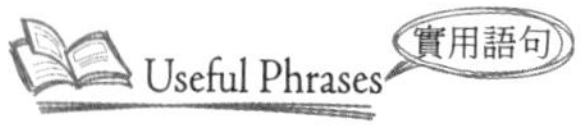

Underground Announcements 地鐵廣播

1. 本次列車 Piccadilly 線開往 Heathrow 機場1、2、3號航站。

   This is a Piccadilly Line service to Heathrow Terminals 1, 2, and 3.

2. 這是經過 Paddington 站及 Baker Street 站的 Circle 線列車。

   This is a Circle Line train via Paddington and Baker Street.

3. 本次列車 Circle 線經過 Tower Hill 站及 Embankment 站。

   This is a Circle Line train via Tower Hill and Embankment.

4. 這是開往 Seven Sisters 的 Victoria 線列車。

   This is a Victoria Line train to Seven Sisters.

5. 這是開往 Richmond 的 District 線列車。

   This is a District Line train to Richmond.

6. 本次列車終點站是 Stratford。

   This train terminates at Stratford.

7. 請隨時顧好個人行李。

   Please keep your luggage with you at all times.

8. 請勿靠近即將關閉的車門！

   Stand clear of the closing doors!

9. 請換車。這是本班列車的終點站。請換車。

   All change please! This train will now terminate here. All change please.

10. 請勿靠近車門！

    Please stand clear of the doors!

11. 請立刻進入車廂。

    Please move right down inside the car!

12. 本班列車就要開了。請注意車門！

    This train is ready to leave. Please mind the doors!

13.謝謝乘坐 Central 線。

Thank you for travelling on the Central Line.

14.倫敦地鐵為延誤的列車致歉。

London Underground apologise for the delay to this service.

4.5 Signs in London Underground 倫敦地鐵標誌

1

Priority seat 博愛座

for people who are disabled, pregnant or less able to stand.

讓位給殘疾人士、孕婦及行動不便者。

2

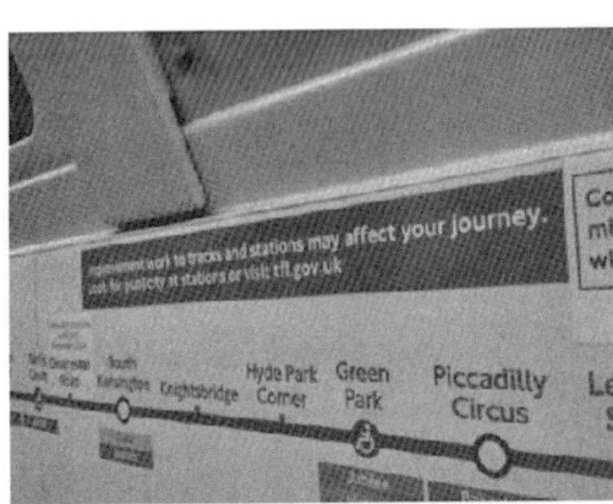

Improvement work to tracks and stations may affect your journey. Look for publicity at stations or visit tfl.gov.uk.
軌道及車站修復工作會耽誤你的行程。注意車站公告及網站 tfl.gov.uk 信息。（tfl 是 Transport for London 倫敦交通網址，讀者去倫敦一定會經常使用這個交通網站。）

3

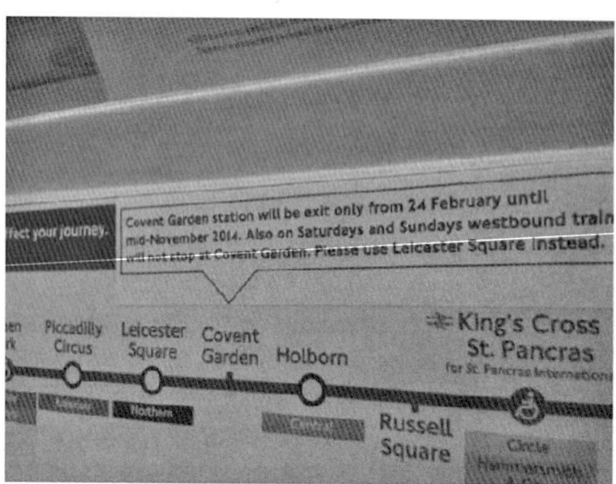

Covent Garden station will be exit only from 24 February until mid-November 2014. Also on Saturdays and Sundays westbound train will not stop at Covent Garden. Please use Leicester Square instead.
柯芬園站從 2014 年 2 月 24 日到 11 月中只能出站。所有往西行的班車，週六、日都不停靠柯芬園站。請改在萊斯特廣場站搭車。

4

District Line 路線名：區域線
Westbound 行駛方向：往西行
platforms 3 & 4 乘車月臺：3、4 月臺
Kensington (Olympia), Ealing Broadway, Richmond, Wimbledon 停靠站名

5

Door alarmed 車門設有警報器
Keep clear 保持淨空
Access required at all times 隨時保持暢通
Fire extinguisher located in drivers cab 滅火器在駕駛室
£80 penalty fare or prosecution if you fail to show on demand a valid ticket for the whole of your journey or a validated Oyster card.
無法出示全程有效車票或有效的牡蠣卡，罰款 80 英鎊並會遭到起訴。

6

CCTV cameras in operation 閉路電視監視中
This scheme is controlled by London Underground. 本計畫由倫敦地鐵執行。
For further information contact 0845 330 9880 詳情電 0845 330 9880

7

Please keep your bags with you at all times and report any unattended items or suspicious behaviour to a member of staff.
請隨時將自己的包包顧好，發現有無人看管的物品或可疑的行為，通報管理人員。

8

Video Cameras 攝影機

For your added security video cameras are being introduced on London Underground trains. People who assault our staff or vandalise our property will be prosecuted.

為加強您的安全，倫敦地鐵車廂啓用攝影機。攻擊員工或損毀公物會遭到起訴。

9

If you see a train being vandalised call the British Transport Police on 0800 40 50 40.

in an emergency dial 999

見到列車遭到破壞，撥打英國交通警察 0800 40 50 40。

緊急事故撥打 999

10

Items trapped in the doors cause delays.
夾在門中的物品會導致延誤。
Please keep your belongings and clothing clear of the doors.
請將您個人的物品及衣服移開車門。

11

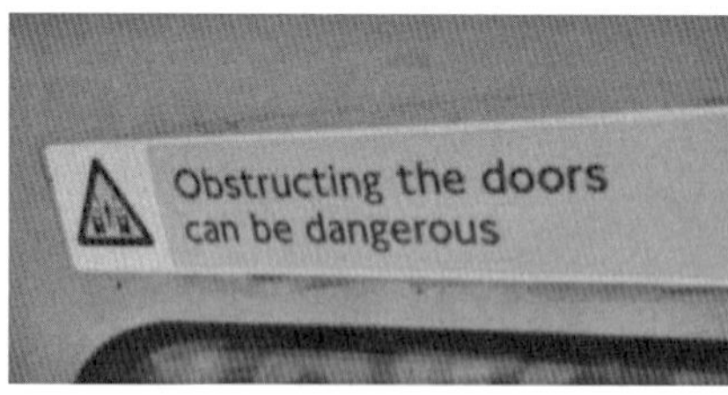

Obstructing the doors can be dangerous.
阻擋車門危險。

12

Platform 0 to 8 月臺 0 到 8
Taxis 計程車
Way out 出口
Dining & Seating 餐飲及休息區
Telephenes 電話

Gates A8-23 A8-23 登機門
B and C gates B 及 C 登機門
Seating areas 休息區

Unit 5 Leisure Activities

休閒活動

住在英國可做的休閒活動很多，無論是參觀博物館、美術館、歷史豪宅，皆可幫助我們了解英國文化，融入英國社會。當然，旅居英國必定要看一齣莎士比亞（William Shakespeare, 1645-1616）的戲劇演出。英國有長遠的戲劇傳統，小學生每學期都會在課堂演出莎翁名劇。英國許多著名的電影明星，都是演莎劇出身，而 Shakespearean Actor（莎劇演員）這個名詞，是優秀演員的品質保證。看一齣莎劇，社交場合必會找到與人交談的話題。對古典音樂有興趣的朋友，可在 The Royal Albert Hall（皇家阿爾伯特音樂廳）聽一場由 BBC 策劃的年度古典音樂節 BBC Proms (http://www.bbc.co.uk/proms)，參觀該音樂廳的建築，感受一下現場觀眾熱烈的氣氛。旅居英國多多參加藝文活動，生活不會孤單無聊，也會交到許多志同道合的英國友人。

5.1 Going to the Theatre
看戲

A: Is there anything on at the theatre this week?	**A:** 劇院本週上演什麼戲？
B: Shakespeare's *Hamlet*.	**B:** 莎士比亞的《哈姆雷特》。
A: Who is in the play?	**A:** 演員是誰？
B: I don't know but I will try to find out on the website.	**B:** 我不知道，但我可以上網查一下。
A: What type of production is it?	**A:** 是哪一類作品？
B: It's a tragedy.	**B:** 是悲劇。
A: Have you seen it before?	**A:** 你以前有看過嗎？
B: Yes, a long time ago.	**B:** 有，很久以前。

A: What time does the performance start?	**A:** 節目何時開始？
B: It starts at 7:30.	**B:** 7:30 開始。
A: What time does it finish?	**A:** 何時結束？
B: I think it finishes around 10 o'clock.	**B:** 大約 10:00。
A: Would you like a programme?	**A:** 你要節目表嗎？
B: Yes, I'd like to know something about this production.	**B:** 好的。我想對這次的演出多了解一點。

A: Are you doing anything on Saturday?	**A:** 你週六有空嗎？
B: No, nothing special.	**B:** 沒什麼特別的事。
A: I was thinking of going to a show. Do you want to come?	**A:** 我想去看戲，你要來嗎？

B: Yes, great. I'd love to.

B: 好啊，我樂意。

A: Do you fancy seeing *Ma Ma Mia*?

A: 你想看《媽媽咪呀》嗎？

B: OK. Do you think we'll be able to get tickets?

B: 好的，但能買到票嗎？

A: Sure, no problem. I'll book them.

A: 沒問題，我來訂票。

B: Oh, brilliant. Will they be very expensive?

B: 太好了。會很貴吧？

A: They won't be cheap. But I'll get the tickets and you can pay for dinner afterwards.

A: 不便宜。我買票，看完戲你請吃飯。

B: What time does it start?

B: 何時開演？

A: At 7:45. Where shall we meet?

A: 7:45 開演，我們在哪見面？

B: What about outside the tube station?

B: 地鐵站外面如何？

A: No, let's meet outside the National Opera House. That way we won't miss each other.

A: 我們還是在國家歌劇院門口見。這樣才不會找不到。

B: Fine. What time?

B: 好的，幾點鐘？

A: At 7 o'clock, so we can have a drink before it starts.

A: 7 點鐘，這樣我們可以在開演前先喝個飲料。

B: Great. See you there.

B: 太好了，到時見。

A: Can I help you?

A: 要幫忙嗎？

B: Yes. I'd like two tickets for *Les Miserables* for Saturday Matinee.

B: 我要買兩張星期六下午場的《悲慘世界》。

A: For this Saturday, the 24th?

A: 本週六，24日，對吧？

B: That's right.

B: 是的。

A: Where do you want them? We've got stalls and balcony.

A: 你要哪裡的位子？我們有一樓大廳及樓上的位子。

B: What's the difference?

B: 有何不同？

A: The stalls are downstairs and they are more expensive. The balcony is upstairs and it's a bit cheaper.

A: 一樓大廳的票比較貴。樓上的票比較便宜。

B: How much are the seats in the stalls?

B: 一樓大廳的位子多少錢？

A: They are £54 pounds each.

A: 一張 54 英鎊。

B: And the balcony?

B: 樓上呢？

A: £28.

A: 28 英鎊。

B: OK, I'll have two stall seats then.

B: 好，我買兩張一樓的位子。

A: How would you like to pay?

A: 如何付款？

B: By credit card. Mastercard.

B: 信用卡，萬事達卡。

A: Can you sign here, please? Thanks. Here you are. Two tickets for Saturday Martinee.

A: 請在此簽名。謝謝。這是兩張週六下午場的票。

B: Thanks very much.

B: 非常感謝。

Dialogue4 對話4

A: Tell me about Shakespeare's Globe.

A: 請講一下莎士比亞的環球劇場。

B: The Globe is a recreation of Shakespeare's theatre built in 1599.

B: 環球劇場是 1599 年建造的莎士比亞娛樂劇場。

A: What happens in the Globe?

A: 環球劇場有什麼活動？

B: We do about 300 performances every year. We do a variety of plays by Shakespeare.

B: 我們每年有 300 多場演出。我們上演各種不同的莎劇。

A: Do you think Shakespeare is still relevant today?

A: 你認為今天莎士比亞對我們有相關性嗎？

B: More than ever. Shakespeare speaks to us about personal feelings, our love, about grief, about joy, about jealousy.

B: 比任何時代都相關。莎士比亞告訴我們什麼是個人情感、什麼是愛情、悲傷、歡樂、嫉妒。

5.2 Visit a Museum
參觀博物館

A: Can you recommend any places to see?

A: 你建議參觀哪些地方？

B: The Natural History Museum is worth a visit.

B: 自然歷史博物館值得一看。

A: Please tell me something about the museum.

A: 請介紹一下這個博物館。

B: This museum is based at 48 Doughty Street in London. It is where Dickens lived for 2 years.

B: 這個博物館位於倫敦 Doughty Street 48 號。狄更斯曾在此住了兩年。

A: What are your most important pieces?

A: 你們最重要的收藏是什麼？

B: We have original manuscript material from *Oliver Twist*. We have the desk that Dickens wrote on for his final novel.

B: 我們有《孤雛淚》小說的原著手稿資料。我們也有狄更斯用來寫最後一本小說的桌子。

A: Dickens was born 200 years ago. Do you think he is still relevant today?

A: 狄更斯生於 200 年前。你認為他跟我們有關聯嗎？

B: Definitely. The things that Dickens was writing about – social inequality, poverty – are still very relevant today.

B: 絕對有。狄更斯描寫的社會不公、貧窮，都跟現在有關。

5.3 Visit The Royal Albert Hall 參觀皇家阿爾伯特音樂廳

A: This is such an incredible building. Tell me about it.

A: 這棟建築真是不可思議，介紹一下。

B: The Royal Albert Hall is the world's most famous stage and it is 140 years old.

B: 皇家阿爾伯特音樂廳是世界最有名的舞臺。已有 140 年的歷史了。

A: What is your favourite thing about the Royal Albert Hall?

A: 你最喜歡皇家阿爾伯特音樂廳的地方？

B: Seeing the audience reaction while walking in for the first time.

B: 觀察首次來訪的觀衆，走進來的反應。

5.4 Visit Kew Gardens
參觀皇家植物園

A: What time does Kew Gardens open?	**A:** 皇家植物園幾點開門？
B: It opens daily at 9:30 am.	**B:** 每天上午 9:30 開門。
A: What time does it close?	**A:** 何時關門？
B: Different areas of Kew Gardens close at different times. Please check details before your visit.	**B:** 花園內不同的區域有不同的關門時間。來訪前請先查好時間。
A: Which station do I get off at?	**A:** 在哪一站下車？
B: Visitors travelling by London Underground can use the Kew Garden station.	**B:** 乘坐倫敦地鐵的訪客可以在皇家植物園站下車。

5.5 Day Trip to Stately Homes
歷史豪宅一日遊

A: Where can I take photographs?

A: 哪裡可以拍照？

B: We welcome amateur photography out of doors.

B: 我們歡迎戶外業餘攝影。

A: Can I use mobile phones to take pictures of the house?

A: 我可以用手機在室內拍照嗎？

B: The use of mobile phones with built-in cameras is permitted indoors (no flash please.)

B: 手機中的相機可以在室內拍照（但不能用閃光燈）。

A: What may I touch?

A: 哪些展示品可以觸摸？

B: We'd love you to be able to touch as much as possible, but many objects are simply too fragile to be handled.

B: 我們願意盡量讓訪客觸摸，可是有些物品太脆弱了，不能碰。

A: Why is it dark inside some historic rooms?

A: 為何歷史建築的室內都很暗？

B: This is to slow down the deterioration of light-sensitive contents, especially textiles and watercolour paintings. We recommend that you allow time for your eyes to adapt to these darker conditions.

B: 這是為了減緩對光亮敏感物品的損壞，如紡織品及水彩畫。我們建議花點時間讓眼睛慢慢適應較黑暗的狀況。

A: Why is it so cold inside some houses in winter?

A: 豪宅內冬天為何都很冷？

B: The heating systems in these houses were not designed for the levels of domestic heating that we have become used to in our own houses. We suggest that you dress warmly.

B: 豪宅內的供暖系統設計跟我們習慣的家用暖氣熱度是不同的。我們建議您多穿衣服保暖。

A: May I use my mobile?

A: 我可以用手機嗎？

B: We'd be really grateful if you could turn off your mobile or put it in silent before going into one of our houses.

B: 進豪宅前若能將手機關機或靜音，我們會很感激。

A: Where may I sit down?

A: 有可以坐的地方嗎？

B: We want you to be able to rest and relax, so we are increasing the seating in our houses.

B: 希望你們能休息及放鬆，我們正在增加豪宅內的椅子。

Stately Home / Country House 貴族鄉間豪宅

I live in the country, but I have a flat in London. 我住在鄉間，在倫敦有一間公寓。

I live in London, but I have a stately home in the country. 我住在倫敦，但在鄉間有一棟房子。

說這兩句話的人不是一般普通的英國人，而是世襲的有頭銜的貴族。因此所謂 Country House 鄉間的房子，不是我們想像的小茅屋，而是一座有歷史價値、幾個世紀家族留傳下來的豪華住宅。擁有這些豪宅的貴族，通常在倫敦也有房屋，這樣他們可以往返城市與鄉村之間。這些占地廣闊的豪宅，皆爲當時享有盛名的建築師所設計，因此在建築上有特殊的歷史風格。豪宅內奢華的室內設計，代代相傳的古董家具、雕像、繪畫等藝術作品，處處展現豪宅主人的財富與藝術品味。環繞豪宅的四周，有寬闊的草坪、可垂釣的河流、依據宅主喜愛所建造的田野景觀及特殊園藝風格的花園。善於經營的貴族，將房間改成旅館、承辦婚宴，並利用農莊自製農產品，賣給遊客，這對維護龐大開銷的豪宅不無小補。而英國從南到北大小不一的 Country Houses 是英國文化遺產及觀光資源最爲重要及豐富的一環。

一般英國人在本國旅遊，參觀富麗堂皇的 Stately Homes / Country Houses 有其長遠的歷史傳統。讀者旅居英國要 Do as the Romans Do.（入境隨俗），找機會參觀一兩座豪門宅第。到底 Stately Homes / Country Houses 有哪些特色吸引英國人或來自其他各地的遊客？

參觀貴族鄉間占地廣大的豪宅分兩個部分：(1) 豪宅外觀建築風格及內部房間陳設與藝術收藏；(2) 廣大遼闊的綠地、田野景觀及花園。在此選兩段豪宅的描述，讀者會了解爲何 Stately Homes 會成爲大眾觀光景點。有興趣的讀者可在這個網站上找到更多有關豪宅的資訊：http://www.stately-homes.com/

(1) Chatsworth House

英國最有名、建築宏偉、經營最好的貴族豪宅是位於英國北方的 Derbyshire 的 Chatsworth House（http://www.chatsworth.org/attractions/house）。讀者在網站上可看到有關豪宅的家族歷史、藝術收藏、建築特色、戶外景觀等。

Chatsworth is home to the Duke and Duchess of Devonshire, and has been passed down through 16 generations of the Cavendish family. The house architecture and collection have been evolving for five centuries. The house has over 30 rooms to explore, from the magnificent Painted Hall, to the family-used chapel, regal State Rooms, newly restored Sketch Galleries and beautiful Sculpture Gallery.

Chatsworth 是 Devonshire 公爵及公爵夫人的住宅，從 Cavendish 家族歷經 16 代傳承下來。豪宅建築及藝術收藏歷經五個世紀。豪宅內有 30 個房間可供參觀，有彩繪大廳、家庭小教堂、莊嚴的貴賓廳、及最新整修完成的素描畫廊及美麗的雕像藝廊。

Chatsworth has one of Europe's most significant art collections. The diverse collection is continually added to, encompassing Old Masters to contemporary ceramics and artefacts from Ancient Egypt, through to cutting edge modern sculpture and computer portraits.

Chatswroth 藏有歐洲最重要的藝術品。收藏品持續增加，包括早期的大師作品到近期的陶瓷藝術、上至古埃及的工藝品到現代的雕刻及電腦畫像。

Chatsworth House sits close to the River Derwent in 1,000 acres of parkland. The large gardens receive 300,000 visitors each year.

位於 Derwent 河上的 Chatsworth House 有 1000 英畝綠地。廣大的花園每年接待 30 多萬遊客。

(2) Gibside landscape park and nature reserve Gibside 景觀公園及自然保護區

Relax, play, explore... for an escape to the country, so close to the city.

Tranquil walks, historic ruins, ever-changing gardens and wildlife-spotting, natural family fun and a new adventure play area, delicious food and tempting shopping－all just a few miles (and easy bus trip) from Newcastle to Gateshead.

舒壓、遊樂、探索……如此臨近城市的鄉間休閒去處。

寧靜步道，歷史遺跡，變化無窮的花園及野生動物的蹤跡，闔家共享的自然野趣，新開設的探險遊樂區，美食及誘人的購物——這一切距離 Newcastle 與 Gateshead，只有短短幾英里（搭公車即可方便抵達）。

Visit www.nationaltrust.org.uk/gibside（網站）

Call 01207 541 820（電話）

註：National Trust 是英國規模龐大的國家自然保育及古蹟保護機構。英國有很多貴族後代將無法維持的豪宅，委託或出售給 National Trust 來接管。

5.6 Travel 旅遊

A: How often do you travel?

A: 你常旅遊嗎？

B: All the time. I am constantly packing and unpacking my suitcases.

B: 常常旅遊。我常常都在打包和拆開行李。

A: What do you need for a perfect holiday?

A: 完美的假期需要什麼？

B: To have people around me, loved ones – be they family or friends.

B: 有我愛的人在我周圍，不管是家人或朋友。

A: Which is your favourite city?

A: 你喜歡的城市？

B: Paris is my favourite place in the world because I spent most of my life there.

B: 巴黎是我喜歡的城市，我大半時間都住在那裡。

A: Your favourite hotel?

A: 你喜歡的旅館？

B: I love Parisian hotels.

B: 我愛巴黎旅館。

A: What do you hate about holidays?

A: 度假令你討厭的地方？

B: Travelling through airports. They can be so crowded, you have to stand in long queues.

B: 在機場奔波。機場人多，要排長隊。

A: Your favourite airline?

A: 你喜歡的航空公司？

B: My favourite one is Air France. I also like British Airways. Their food and service are great.

B: 我最喜歡法國航空。我也喜歡英航。他們的餐飲及服務都很好。

A: What is your best piece of travel advice?

A: 你最好的旅遊建議？

B: Pack everything you might need.

B: 可能會用到的都裝進行李。

A: What has travelling taught you?

A: 旅遊學到什麼？

B: About different cultures and how people are different in every country, from how they eat to what their family values are. I always try to learn a few words from a new language wherever I travel.

B: 認識不同文化，不同的國家不一樣的人，從食物到家庭價值觀。我旅遊時，都會從一個新的語言學幾個字。

A: Where next?

A: 下個旅遊地點？

B: If I get a chance this year, I'd love to spend some time in Asia.

B: 今年有機會，很想去亞洲玩。

旅居英國，度假是生活的必需品。一般英國人都會及早為每年兩週的假期計畫安排。在沒有網路科技的年代，Travel Agency / Travel Agent（如 Thomas Cook 等旅行社）是旅遊資訊的重要來源。現在雖然可以透過網站自行安排旅遊，還是有不少英國人喜歡找 Travel Agent 幫忙訂機票旅館，或購買旅行社的套裝行程。旅行社雖有網站但也需要印製精美、圖文並茂的宣傳手冊（brochures），供顧客參考。以下是英國一家旅遊公司 Superbreak 推出的倫敦之旅簡介。讀者嘗試熟悉英文地名及專有名詞，不需中文翻譯。

5 steps to plan your perfect London break 規劃完美倫敦假期的五步驟

1 Where am I going to stay? 住在哪裡？

Superbreak offers over 275 two to five star hotels.

Superbreak 有超過 275 家兩星到五星級的旅館可供選擇。

2 How am I going to travel? 交通的選擇？

Superbreak offers low cost Rail and Coach Travel options as well as Oyster cards to make getting around by bus and tube both easy and inexpensive.

Superbreak 安排您搭乘便宜的火車或客運，並提供倫敦運輸系統的儲值卡牡蠣卡，讓您輕鬆省錢地乘坐公車和地鐵四處遊玩。

3 What am I going to do? 有什麼好玩的？

Superbreak provides so many options that it is impossible to list them all. Theatre, Rock, Pop and Classical Concerts, Opera and Ballet, Exhibitions, Private Tours to Historical Royal Palaces and a host of attractions that will enable you to fill your days and nights.

Superbreak 提供的選擇多到難以一一列出。戲劇、搖滾、流行音樂、古典音樂會、歌劇、芭蕾舞、展覽、歷史皇宮的個人導覽，還有很多其他可看可玩的，讓您白天、夜間同樣充實。

4 How am I going to book? 如何預訂？

Superbreak offers you three choices: Superbreak 提供三種選購方式：

(1) Research and book online at www.superbreak.com. 前往 www.superbreak.com 網站瀏覽資料直接預訂。

(2) Call our experienced friendly staff – available on 0871 221 1199. 直撥 0871 221 1199 給我們經驗豐富又友善的專員。

(3) See your local Travel Agent. 找您當地的旅行社代辦。

The price is the same whichever option you choose. 無論您以何種方式預訂，價格一律相同。

What to do in London 遊倫敦

1 Cultural and Historical London 文化歷史之旅

Choose from more national museums in one city than any other capital in the world.

從眾多國家級博物館中挑選一所參觀，選擇比世界任何一個首都城市都要多。

Explore the largest collection of British art in the world at Tate Britain.

探索收藏英國藝術品最豐富的美術館－Tate Britain。

Take in a Shakespearean play at Shakespeare's Globe, in the area where he lived and worked.

前往莎士比亞過去居住工作的地區，在環球劇場看一齣莎劇。

2 Eating and Drinking 美食之旅

Browse at London's oldest food market – Borough Market.

瀏覽倫敦最古老的菜市場－Borough Market。

Take afternoon tea at the Ritz. 到麗池飯店喝下午茶。

3 Shopping 購物之旅

Shop in the UK's leading retail city – more than 40,000 shops and 80 individual markets.

倫敦是英國最大的購物城，有 4 萬家商店及 80 個單獨的市場。

Pick up some royal treats at Fortnum & Mason. The Queen's

grocer.

去女王採買食品的 Fortnum & Mason 挑一點皇家美食。

4 Sights and Experience 景點和體驗

See the world's oldest insect at the Natural History Museum.

到自然歷史博物館看世上最古老的昆蟲。

Stand where time begins, on the Greenwich Meridian Line at the Royal Observatory.

去皇家天文臺，站在時間的起點，格林威治子午線上。

Unit 6 Healthcare

醫療

The National Health Service 簡稱 NHS 是英國健保署，等同我們的全民健保。英國民眾很驕傲肯定 NHS 醫療制度，雖然不是萬分滿意。抵達英國，找到住處，就可到附近的診所登記註冊家醫。英國健保署的網站上（http://www.nhs.uk）有詳盡的醫療資訊，也提供許多健身錄影節目，方便大眾上網做健身運動。生病可預約看家醫，但常常要等候數日。平常很多小病如感冒、咳嗽、頭痛、腹瀉等，可找藥劑師（pharmacists）開藥，節省時間。在英國的醫療制度上，合格的藥劑師提供醫藥咨詢服務，他們也會建議你是否需要看專科醫師。英國最大的醫藥百貨藥局 Boots（http://www.boots-uk.com/）有 2500 家大小不等的分店，遍布全國各大購物中心、商店街及社區小鎮，為民眾提供專業便利的服務。

6.1 Registering with a GP
登記家醫

A: How can I register with my local GP?

A: 如何跟當地的家醫註冊？

B: When you arrive in the UK you should register with your nearest doctor, also known as a General Practitioner (GP). This will allow you to access the UK's healthcare system. To find your nearest GP, visit the NHS website below and enter your postcode, town name or area. On the website you can also find your nearest surgery, emergency and urgent care centre, hospital, dentist, pharmacy and eye doctor.

B: 抵達英國應跟就近的醫師註冊，也就是你的家庭醫師。這樣你可登入健保系統。你可在全國健保的網站上輸入你的郵遞區號或市區地名，就可找到最近的診所、急診看護中心、醫院、牙科、藥房及眼科醫師。

A: How do I find a dentist?

A: 如何找到牙醫？

B: The National Health Service (NHS) provides dental care and it is available to everyone, even if you are not registered with the NHS.

B: 全國健保服務提供牙齒保健給所有的人，沒有登記 NHS 的人亦可利用。

6.2 At the Chemist's
藥局

A: Can I help you?	**A:** 要幫忙嗎？
B: Yes, I cut my finger yesterday, and it really hurts.	**B:** 是的。我昨天割到手指，很痛。
A: You need some antiseptic cream.	**A:** 你需要消毒藥膏。
B: OK. Could I have some plasters, please?	**B:** 好的。我也需要創可貼。
A: Yes, of course. That's £6.95.	**A:** 好的。共 6.95 英鎊。

A: How can I help?	**A:** 能幫忙嗎？
B: I need something for a cold.	**B:** 我需要感冒藥。

A: Right, try these tablets – they are very good.

A: 好，試試這些藥片一很有效。

B: Ok, and how often do I take them?

B: 好的。多久服用一次？

A: Take two tablets every four hours with water.

A: 配水每四小時吃兩粒。

B: Thanks. Can I have some cough medicine, please?

B: 謝了。我也需要咳嗽藥。

1. 你應該去看家醫。
   You should go and see your GP.
2. 我不舒服。有發燒。
   I don't feel very well. I've got a temperature.
3. 你應去藥店。
   You should go to a chemist's.
4. 你應在床上躺一兩天。
   You should stay in bed for a day or two.

Unit 7 Entertaining BBC TV Programmes

BBC有趣的電視節目

旅居英國，想要與人溝通，看英國人愛看的電視節目最容易找到話題。本單元電視節目選自英國廣播公司 BBC（British Broadcasting Company），觀看這些高水準的娛樂節目，可以學到實用又生活化的英語。BBC 標榜的目標有三：to inform（提供資訊），to educate（教育），to entertain（娛樂）；重要的服務項目有：電視、廣播電臺、及網站（www.bbc.co.uk）。BBC 透過 iPlayer 系統提供民眾 catch-up TV service 線上或手機上補看遺漏節目。在節目製作上，BBC 堅持 Putting quality first（品質優先），因此節目沒有廣告，保證 viewing quality（觀看品質）。為服務聽障觀眾，電視節目都有提供 subtitle（英語字幕）。對我們來說，看字幕可幫助我們了解內容，久了，聽力也就進步了。我選了四種不同類型的電視節目：古董拍賣、法拍屋、烹飪競賽、購買鄉間住宅。讀者可學到各種情境的 Authentic English（真實英語對話）。旅居英國若能經常觀看電視節目，不但可以增進英語能力，更是融入英國社會文化最直接的途徑。

7.1 Flog It
古董拍賣

BBC One 播出的 *Flog It* 是屬於古董節目（Antiques Show）類型，每日下午 4:30 播出，2002 年播出至今。flog 照字面解釋是「鞭打」，此處指古董拍賣使用的錘子（hammer），錘子敲下表示拍賣成交。節目模式分兩部分，在不同的現場拍攝。(1) 節目主持人到全國各地選定製作節目的地點，邀請當地民衆將家中收在閣樓或櫃櫥的古董拿到節目現場，由古董專家代為鑑定寶物的年代、特點、估價。(2) 節目主持人在衆多鑑定過的古董中，選定七樣特殊古董，拿到當地的古董拍賣公司進行拍賣，並與古董主人及古董專家共同觀看拍賣過程。節目最吸引觀衆的就是民衆家中不起眼或遺忘的古董，被行家或博物館看中，高價收買。

（這是節目的片頭）

閱讀本節目的情境對話，讀者可得到很多有關英國文化的知識。一般英國人家中都有一點祖傳的寶物（不一定値錢），透過對寶物的描述，讀者可以學到很多描述事物的形容詞，如表達驚奇用語：fantastic, amazing, unbelievable, incredible, gorgeous, thrilled 等。

A: Tell me a little bit about its history. Is this a family piece?

A: 講一下這件寶物的來歷。是家產吧？

B: It was a family piece, but I am the end of the family chain.

B: 是家產，但我是最後一代。

A: Who did it belong to first?

A: 最先是屬於誰的？

B: It would have been my grandmother and when she died, my mother inherited it when I was very young so it's always been in my life.

B: 是我祖母的，她過世後，傳給我母親，從我小時候，它就一直跟著我。

A: What have you done with it? Have you had this on the wall?

A: 你如何處理？掛在牆上嗎？

B: I've had it on the wall. I took it off this morning.

B: 掛在牆上。今早取下。

A: Why are you selling it?

A: 為何要賣掉？

B: I don't like brown wood furniture.

B: 我不喜歡棕色的木製家具。

A: Whereabouts is it stood in the house?

A: 放在家中何處？

B: In the spare room. So it is not in view.

B: 空房間。這樣看不到它。

A: Why are you selling it?

A: 為何要賣掉？

B: We're downsizing and we want to get a bungalow. So we've got to get rid of some of the stuff that's stuck in our loft.

B: 我們要精簡家當，搬到平房，所以要處理閣樓中的物品。

Dialogue 3 對話3

A: Where have they come from?

A: 從哪裡得到的？

B: We found them in the back of an aunt's cupboard when she died.

B: 我嬸嬸過世後，在櫃櫥後面找到的。

A: Why do you want to sell it?

A: 為何要賣掉？

B: It's really hard to display in a house. My children are grown up, neither of them were interested in these things.

B: 家中找不到擺設的地方。小孩也長大了，對古董不感興趣。

A: Do you have any expectations?

A: 你有期待拍賣的價錢？

B: I hope it would be about £200.

B: 我希望能賣到200英鎊。

A: Tell me about this lovely snuff box that you've brought in today.

A: 告訴我有關你今天帶來的精巧鼻煙壺。

B: It always sat on my parent's chest of drawers in the bedroom. I inherited it and it was sitting on my chest of drawers.

B: 它一直都放在我父母臥房的五斗櫃中。傳給了我，也放在那裡。

A: Why do you want to get rid of it?

A: 你為何不要了？

B: I have two sons and neither of them want it.

B: 我有兩個兒子，他們都不要它。

A: Why have you brought it to show me today?

A: 你今天為何帶這個來給我看？

B: I'd like to know how much it's worth.

B: 我想知道它值多少錢。

A: How did you come by them?

A: 你從哪得來的？

B: They were a present to me about 30 years ago, and I've never used them, they've always been stored.

B: 30 年前有人送給我這個禮物，我從未用過，一直都存放著。

A: They are unfashionable but at the same time, they are pretty, they are over 100 years old. I am going to put an estimate of £50 to £80 on them. I think we need to protect them with a reserve.

A: 目前這東西不流行，但它們很漂亮，有 100 年之久。我估價 50 到 80 英鎊。我們應放最低保護價。

A: Where did you buy it from?

A: 你在哪兒買的？

B: Just from the local charity shop recently.

B: 就在家附近的慈善商店。

A: So somebody brought this in as a donation?

A: 所以是有人捐贈的。

B: Yes, that's correct.

B: 對的。

A: How much did you pay for it in your charity shop?

A: 你在慈善商店花了多少錢買的？

B: Only £10.

B: 10 英鎊而已。

Dialogue 7 對話7

A: Whose is it? Is it yours?

A: 這是誰的？是你的嗎？

B: My great grandparents.

B: 我曾祖父母的。

A: So it's been in the family all the time.

A: 所以是傳家之寶。

B: Five generations and me the end of the line.

B: 傳了五代，我是最後一代。

A: Where did you get this from?

A: 你從哪得到這個東西？

B: It's not mine, it's my son's. He bought it in an antiques fair.

B: 不是我的，是我兒子的。他在古董市場買的。

A: How much did he pay for it?

A: 他花了多少錢？

B: I think he paid about £150 for it. He had his eye on it and he asked me for the cash.	**B:** 我想他花了 150 英鎊。他看中了，向我要錢。
A: I would say, auction estimate on this would be about £250 to £350. How does that sound to you?	**A:** 我猜拍賣估錢大約是 250 到 350 英鎊。你認為如何？
B: That sounds good to me.	**B:** 很好。
A: Has your son just got into antiques, or has he been doing this for a while?	**A:** 你兒子剛開始對古董有興趣，還是玩古董有一段時間了？
B: He started when he was about 12. He's got an interest in silver. He'd like to be a dealer or possibly an auctioneer.	**B:** 他 12 歲開始就對銀器感興趣。他想做古董生意或拍買商。
A: How old is he now?	**A:** 他現在幾歲？
B: He's 15 now. He has got a brilliant eye.	**B:** 他現年 15 歲，很有眼光。
A: Let's put an estimate of £250 – £350, with a £250 reserve.	**A:** 我們可估價 250 到 350 英鎊，訂 250 英鎊為最低拍賣價。

A: Tell me about its history.

A: 告訴我它的來歷。

B: They were given to me by a neighbour of my mother's. She was quite elderly. When she passed away, she left them to me in her will.

B: 是我母親的鄰居給我的。她年紀很大了。過世後，她在遺囑中留給我。

A: They lived at home?

A: 它們一直都放在家中嗎？

B: They've been packed up and on top of my wardrobe.

B: 我把它們包起來放在衣櫥上面。

A: If they make a lot of money, would you put it towards another form of antique or something brand new?

A: 若他們能賺錢，你會再買不一樣的古董還是買新東西？

B: I'd probably have my gardens done. I bought the house off the neighbour after she passed away and I decorated all the inside of the house and I would like to do the gardens.

B: 我也許會整理花園。鄰居過世後我買了她的房子。房內已裝修好，花園還要整理。

A: Why do you want to sell them?

A: 為何要賣？

B: They're just sitting in my cupboard doing nothing.

B: 它們擺在櫥櫃中沒用。

A: Are these yours?

A: 是你的嗎？

B: Yes, I used to love playing with them as a child.

B: 是的，是我小時候愛玩的東西。

A: We need to protect your interests with a reserve.

A: 我們需要定最低拍賣價，以維護你的利益。

Dialogue 11 對話11

A: Did it belong to your parents?

A: 它是你父母的嗎？

B: It did.

B: 是的。

A: How much did you pay for that?

A: 你花了多少錢買的？

B: It was about £200 about 20 years ago.

B: 20 年前要 200 英鎊。

A: Why are you thinking of selling them?

A: 你為何要賣？

B: We are downsizing.

B: 我們正在精簡家當。

A: Can you tell our viewers something about internet bidding?

A: 你能對電視觀衆說說有關線上競拍嗎？

B: The internet opened the market worldwide, which is good. It's good for the vendors, it's good all round, really. Without the internet, there would be no such thing as worldwide connection, would there? You wouldn't find the buyers in America or Canada or Australia.

B: 網路開放了世界市場，是件好事。對賣主好，對大家都好。沒有網路，世界就不會連結在一起，對吧？你也不會找到在美國、加拿大或澳洲的買主。

A: How do we bid online?

A: 如何線上競拍？

B: Obviously when you're bidding online, you've got to book the line in advance.

B: 當然了，線上競拍要預先登記。

A: What happens when you're on a computer?

A: 電腦上線後做什麼？

住所 平面媒體與通訊 日常生活 交通 休閒活動 醫療 BBC有趣的電視節目 閱讀廣告 附錄

B: Basically, you've got a webcam on me, and I'm microphoned up. They will register online on their computer, their laptop, they put all their details in, we check their credit card details against their address to make sure they're genuine. They literally can see me, they can hear me, and at the click of a mouse, they can bid.

B: 簡單說，你在網路攝影機會看到我，我戴了麥克風。上網競標的人都要線上註冊，填寫個人資料。我們會核對他們的信用卡及地址，確定實名。上線的人都可以看到我、聽到我，只要按滑鼠就可競標了。

A: Thank you.

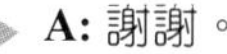

A: 謝謝。

節目中經常出現的語句，都是一般英國人談話常用的句子，非常實用，值得讀者練習。

1. 告訴我從哪來的？
   Tell me where did you get them?
2. 為何要賣？
   Why are you selling it?
3. 錢怎麼用？
   What do you do with the money?
4. 為何要清除雜物？
   Why do you want to declutter?
5. 你知道這位藝術家嗎？
   Do you know anything about the artist?
6. 你滿意嗎？
   Are you happy with that?
7. 錢要用在什麼地方？
   What will you put the money towards?

8. 有什麼可拍賣的？

What can we bring to flog?

9. 找到有趣的東西嗎？

Have you found anything interesting?

10. 可以訂個最低價嗎？

Could we put a reserve on that?

11. 願意賣嗎？

Are you happy to sell it?

12. 為何買這個？

Why did you buy it?

13. 記得花了多少錢嗎？

Can you remember how much you paid for it?

14. 知道這是誰的嗎？

Do you know who owned this?

15. 錢你們會平分嗎？

Are you going to split the money?

16. 你知道雕刻家是誰嗎？

Do you know who the carver was?

17. 它在櫃櫥裡。

It sits in the cabinet.

18. 有別人喜歡它就更好了。

It would be nice for someone else to enjoy it.

19. 我們帶到拍賣場。

Let's take them to auction.

20. 謝謝你帶這個來。

Thank you for bringing it along.

21. 一定要把這個拍賣掉。

It has got to go under the hammer.

22. 我們仔細看一下。

Let's look at it a little closely.

23. 你不喜歡繪畫。

You are not a big fan of this painting.

24.定一個低的保留價是對的。

It's wise to have that low reserve.

25.我會帶家人去飯館吃頓飯。

I'll take the family out for a meal.

26.真有眼光。

Spot on.

27.看到這個可愛的小人像，我很興奮。

I was so excited when I looked at these lovely little figures.

28.雕刻的品質非常美麗、細緻、精確。

The quality of carving is so beautiful, so refined and so precise.

29.那很好。我覺得 80 英鎊的最低保留價是很合理的。

That would be nice. I would feel that a reserve of £ 80 might be the most reasonable.

30.希望它們在能在拍賣會上有好成績。

Let's hope that they will do well at the auction.

31.謝謝你帶來這銀器，希望當天會有銀器專家在場。

Thank you so much for bringing them in and hopefully the silver buyers will be there on the day.

32.它特別吸引我。

It particularly appealed to me.

33.你的東西可以賣給喜愛的收藏家。

It could go to someone who's a collector and can enjoy it.

34.這些油畫在我手中已有兩年之久。

I've owned these oil paintings for about two years.

35.我媽媽精簡家當時，給了我。

They came into my possession when my mum downsized.

36.太吸引人了。

It is very impressive.

37.天哪！我太吃驚了。

Good Lord, I am amazed.

38.假如這一對沒有瑕疵的話，可賣到 400 到 600 英鎊。因為有瑕疵，要花錢修補。

If they were in good condition, you would be looking at £400 to £600 for the pair. They are in poor condition, they need money spending on them.

39.值得收藏的寶物。

A very collectible object.

40.我認為拍賣價可賣到 60 到 100 英鎊。

I would put an auction estimate of anything from £60 to £100.

41.你也許會找到一個喜愛它的收藏家。

You might find a collector who falls in love with that.

42.場內大爆滿。

It is a packed house.

43.我們要實際一點。

We've got to be realistic.

44.聽起來很合理。

That sounds reasonable to me.

45.它的風格很古典，也很精緻。

It's quite classical in style. It's quite exquisite.

46.這裡有點損壞。損壞是個問題。有點可惜。

There is a little bit of damage here. The damage is a problem. It's a shame.

47.放在家中很久了。

It's been in the family for quite some time.

48.你知道它值多少錢嗎？

Do you have any idea how much it's worth?

49. 我願意賣給會欣賞看重它的人。

I prefer it to go to somebody who would appreciate it.

1. charity shop 慈善（公益）商店：這是英國文化非常重要的一環，讀者旅居英國一定要逛逛這些商店。店內商品多為英國人家中不用的物品、衣服，捐贈給性質不同的慈善機構如：Cancer Research（支助癌症研究）、Oxfam（支援第三世界）、Help the Aged（幫助老年人）等。店內貨品多為捐贈，因此價格非常便宜。英國人認為去 charity shop 買東西是做善事，省錢、環保。也有專賣名牌二手服飾的慈善公益商店，名人也會光顧。
2. bungalow 平房：一般英國人的居住空間會隨著年齡循環。年輕未婚時多住 flat（公寓），有了家及小孩需要更大的空間及房間，改住 semi-detached（雙拼）或 detached（獨棟住宅），上下兩層、有花園。等孩子長大離家後，就 down-size（精簡家當），再搬到平房或公寓。年長者，住平房不需要上下樓梯，住公寓則不需整理花園。
3. loft 屋頂上的閣樓：一般英國人會把家中不用的物品都堆到閣樓中。因此有很多寶物珍藏都是從清理閣樓中無意間發現的。
4. will 遺囑：一般英國人生前都會找律師立遺囑，清理家當，將有價值或有意義的物品指名留給親人或朋友。因此拍賣場上經常會出現來自親友或鄰居遺囑中贈與的古董。

7.2 Homes Under the Hammer
法拍錘下的房屋

Homes Under the Hammer 是 BBC 每日早上十點鐘播出的一小時節目，從 2003 年開播至今，深受觀衆歡迎。從節目的標題「法拍錘下的房屋」讀者可知此類房屋都是破舊（run-down）、房屋有龜裂（crack）、會漏水（leak）、屋內堆了垃圾（litter）。但因拍賣房價比正常市價便宜，因此有人願意買並花時間整修改造。每一集（episode）製作的模式相同：節目主持人（presenter）事

先鎖定幾戶需要大事整修、幾乎無法居住的法拍屋，到拍買現場（auction room）觀看拍賣投標（bid）的過程。隨後主持人拜訪得標屋主，詢問他們得標的價錢、整修房屋的計畫、預算及整修時間，並詢問屋主會面對的棘手問題。

節目開始主持人會說：

All these properties have been sold at auction. We will find out who bought them and what they paid for them when they went under the hammer. We hope we've inspired you on Homes under the Hammer.

本節目所有的房屋都是法拍屋。我們會找到房屋買主，詢問他們得標價錢。希望對你買法拍屋能有所啟發。

主持人訪問屋主的對話包括：屋主的背景、購買法拍屋的動機，改造房屋的可能性（potential）、房屋周遭環境的描述以及房屋的估價。

A: What did you think when you first walked through the door?

A: 你一進門時有何想法？

B: It's big. I wanted to see the size, the layout, what we could do.

B: 房子很大。我要看大小、格局，以及能做什麼。

A: Why did you want to buy it?

A: 為何要買這間法拍屋？

B: It just looked like a fantastic stone-built house which I quite like, and an opportunity because it was wrecked internally.

B: 這棟用石頭建造的房子很棒，是我喜歡的，房子內部損毀，有翻修改造的機會。

A: Do you have any experience of property renovation?

A: 你有住宅改造的經驗嗎？

B: None at all.

B: 完全沒有。

A: Do you think it is a safe investment?

A: 你認為這是個安全的投資嗎？

B: Although the market is going down at the moment, I just think it's much better to have money in property than it is to leave it in the bank.

B: 雖然目前市場不看好，但比起將錢存在銀行，投資房地產還是比較好。

A: How much is that going to cost, do you think?

A: 你想整修需要花多少錢？

B: My budget for the total renovation is about £50,000.

B: 我的總預算是 5 萬英鎊。

A: Any idea how long this is going to take?

A: 有想過整修需要多久的時間嗎？

B: Approximately four weeks.

B: 大約需四週。

A: Who is going to do the work?

A: 誰負責整修的工作？

B: I will be doing most of the work, but the skimming of the ceilings and the carpets will be done by other people I know.

B: 我會負責大部分的工作，但清理天花板及地毯由我認識的人來做。

A: Once you have renovated this gorgeous house, what will you do with it?

A: 整修好這棟華麗的房子，你要如何處理？

B: I think I may sell it.

B: 我可能會出售。

A: When you are not doing property stuff, what do you do?

A: 你不整修房屋時，都做些什麼？

B: I do a lot of internet betting.

B: 我在網上下賭注。

A: What do you do?

A: 你的職業？

B: We are joiners. We are sick of doing houses up for everyone else.

B: 我們是木工。不想再替別人修房屋了。

A: Had you researched this property? Have you viewed it?

A: 你有先查過這個房屋嗎？有先看過嗎？

B: I looked at it on the internet. I did everything on the internet.

B: 我有在網站上看過。我都上網辦事。

A: What made you decide to do this house?

A: 你為何決定整修這棟房子？

B: I've always been a saver and the money I have in the bank is not doing anything. With house prices dropping, we thought now would be the time. It's a wise investment.

B: 我是個儲蓄的人，錢存在銀行沒什麼用。房價在跌，現在正是時候。該是明智的投資。

A: Why this property?

A: 為何選這棟房屋？

B: We've got the resources, it's been quiet at work, so we can spend more time in here.

B: 我們已有資金，目前也沒什麼工作，所以可以多花些時間整修房屋。

A: How much do you think you'll spend?

A: 你預計花費多少？

B: The actual budget is £50,000. We might spend a little bit more over the budget.

B: 確實的預算是 5 萬英鎊。我們可能會比預算多花一些。

A: That's a healthy budget. Did you read the legal pack?

A: 這是個合理的預算。你有看法律資料嗎？

B: No, the solicitor has.

B: 沒有，但律師有看。

A: Is there any problem?

A: 有任何難題嗎？

B: No, we got away with it.

B: 沒有，都解決了。

A: How long will it take you to do the work?

A: 整修要多久？

B: I would reckon about six months.

B: 我猜要六個多月。

A: Are you both property developers?

A: 兩位都是開發房地產的吧？

B: We are trying to be.

B: 我們試著做這一行。

A: So do you have another job as well?

A: 所以你還有其他的工作？

B: I just do the property development side now. I also do engine building once a week.

B: 目前只做房產開發。每週也做引擎組裝。

A: What made you think that you could do a lot with this property?

A: 這棟房子哪裡可大大整修？

B: It's probably the high ceilings.

B: 也許是挑高的天花板。

A: I have to say the layout isn't as it should be. Do you agree?

A: 我認為這屋子的格局不應如此。你同意嗎？

B: I agree. The layout probably needs some work.

B: 同意。格局是要更動的。

A: How long do you think it's going to take you to renovate this place?

A: 整修這個地方需要多久的時間？

B: We could do all the work in four weeks.

B: 所有的工作都會在四週內完成。

A: Would you make another visit to the auction?

A: 你會再去拍賣場買房嗎？

B: Yes, definitely. It's a lot easier to buy from an auction. It's quicker, as well. You don't have the hassle of the estate agents pushing you for more money. When the hammer goes down, it's yours.

B: 肯定會的。買法拍屋很容易，也很快。房屋仲介不會找麻煩，提高價錢。當拍賣鎚敲下，房子就是你的了。

A: How much could the house be worth after renovation?

A: 整修後房屋價值多少？

B: In its current condition, I would anticipate this property to be worth in the region of £35,000－£40,000. Ceiling price, once done to a good standard, would be in the region of £55,000.

B: 依照目前的狀況，我預期這棟房屋的價格大約在 35,000 到 40,000 英鎊之間。假如可做到高水準整修，最高價可賣到 55,000 英鎊左右。

A: How much could he achieve if he sold it?

A: 假如他出售，可賣多少？

B: I would put the property on the market for £289,000.

B: 我會以 289,000 英鎊的價格放在市場上出售此棟房屋。

A: What could a rental return achieve?

A: 出租的話，租金是多少？

B: I would say that we would rent this flat out in the region of £1,000 per calendar month.

B: 我們會以每個月 1,000 英鎊出租這棟公寓。

A: How much rent could this semi generate?

A: 這棟雙拼房屋可租多少？

B: My opinions are, on a rental valuation, once the property has been renovated, it would be worth in the region of £600 per calendar month.

B: 我的建議是，在租金方面，一旦房屋整修後，租金可值每月 600 英鎊左右。

A: If it is put up for sale?

A: 出售價？

B: Once the property has been renovated to a high standard, my estimate for resale value would be in the region of £165,000.

B: 若是這棟房屋改造的水準很高的話，我估計可賣到 165,000 英鎊左右。

A: They spent £230,000, so how much could the flat fetch if sold on?

A: 屋主花了 230,000 英鎊買的話，這棟公寓可賣多少？

B: I think if this flat was to come on the market, it would be in and around £270,000.

B: 假如要賣這棟公寓，目前市場價格大約在 270,000 英鎊左右。

1. 這是很特殊的工作。

   It's a very special job.

2. 我認為這房屋很特別，很有特色，而且正好在小鎮中心。

   I think it is unique, it's characterful and it's set right in the heart of the village.

3. 這會是個很好的買或租的好投資。

   This would certainly make a fantastic buy-to-let investment.

4. 新舊的結合是世界一流的。

The juxtaposition of the old and the new is world class.

5. 房屋的格局非常好。

The layout of the property is very good.

6. 這房子可以用來投資嗎？

Does it work as an investment?

7. 廚房需要換新。

The kitchen needs updating.

8. 第一印象：公寓改造的乾淨俐落。

The first impression of the flat is, it's a nice, clean conversion.

9. 房屋很整齊乾淨，看起來很寬敞。

It's neat and tidy and shows off the space well.

10. 公寓的地點是很好的資產。

The position is also a fantastic asset for the flat.

11. 在拍賣之前，我們看了五棟公寓。

We looked at five flats in total before the auction.

12. 這種房屋有高度需求。

There is a huge demand for this type of property.

13. 廚房絕對需要更換。

The kitchen definitely needs replacing.

14. 你有對這棟房子做過調查嗎？

Have you got a survey on this property?

15. 你買了一戶破舊的排屋。

You bought a run-down terraced house.

16. 整修房屋會出很多差錯。

Plenty can go wrong with property renovation.

17. 我們需要僱用專家幫忙。

We need to employ professional help.

18. 太好了，做得很好。

Brilliant, it's been done very nicely.

19. 可以分成兩間公寓。

You could split it into two flats.

20. 雖然他們很明智的拿了法律資料，可是在拍賣之前，律師沒時間讀。

Although they sensibly obtained the legal pack, the solicitor didn't have time to read it before the auction.

21. 凸窗很漂亮，我喜歡它的顏色。

The bay windows are fantastic and I like the colours.

BBC 製作節目一定遵照其所標榜的目標：傳達資訊、教育功能、娛樂大眾（to inform, to educate, to entertain）。*Homes Under the Hammer* 節目內容緊湊、有高度的娛樂性；更重要的是告知觀眾買法拍屋一定要先閱讀法律資料（legal pack），注意法律規則。改造房屋要有時間及預算的規劃，盡量在預定時間內完成，同時不要超出預算。

節目中主持人與屋主、仲介經理訪談的對話，都是我們旅居英國日常生活常用的語言。熟悉這個節目中經常出現的真實情境對話，不但可以幫助我們理解及欣賞節目內容，了解英國文化，更重要的是，學到的英語是母語人士常用的真實英語（authentic English）。

7.3 Cooking Competition 烹飪大賽

The Great British Bake Off「英國烘焙大賽」及 *Celebrity Masterchef*「名人大廚」是 BBC 高收視率節目。*The Great British Bake Off* 是 2010 年製作的烹飪節目，競賽項目是烘焙糕點。參與競賽的候選人皆為業餘烘焙人士。節目播出以來，深受觀眾歡迎，讀者也可以在有線頻道 BBC Lifestyle 看到這個節目。另一個娛樂性極高的烹飪比賽節

目是 *Celebrity Masterchef* 參賽者是各行業的名人。觀衆喜歡看名人煮菜，當然更喜歡看名人煮菜失敗的過程。
烹飪比賽節目中主持人及參賽者的對話，多圍繞在食材及烹飪步驟的描述。觀看這類節目，學到一些烹飪知識及英語表達方式。此類節目涉及到參賽者的贏輸，因此我們會聽到很多表達驚奇、興奮、失望的語句。這是一般英語會話讀本中學不到的。

A: How are you?

A: 你好嗎？

B: I am very nervous, actually.

B: 事實上，我有些緊張。

A: What are you cooking?

A: 你做哪道菜？

B: We are making Spaghetti Bolognese.

B: 我們做義大利肉醬麵。

A: What are your two dishes?

A: 你的兩道菜是什麼？

B: For my main, I'm going to be doing pan-fried sea bass and chorizo with celeriac puree.

B: 我的主菜是煎海鱸魚及西班牙香腸佐芹菜泥。

A: And your second course?

A: 第二道菜？

B: A chocolate fondant.

B: 熔岩巧克力蛋糕。

A: Are you aware of how many people have lost their place in this competition to a chocolate fondant?

A: 你知道有很多參賽者因為熔岩巧克力蛋糕而失去資格？

B: I'm hoping I can show you that I have a fool-proof way of doing it.

B: 希望我能展示一個簡單安全的做法。

Dialogue 3 對話3

A: What are your two dishes?

A: 你的兩道菜是什麼？

B: Pan-fried lamb's liver with bacon, and then sticky toffee pudding with a pecan sauce.

B: 培根煎羊肝，濃溼的太妃布丁加胡桃醬。

A: So, liver and bacon, absolute classic.

A: 羊肝、培根，絕對是經典配。

B: This dish relies upon the sauce to hold it together.

B: 這道菜要靠醬汁結合。

A: How do you feel about sticky toffee pudding?

A: 你覺得濃溼的太妃布丁甜點如何？

B: I love it. I've made it about twenty times.

B: 我很喜歡。我做過 20 多次。

A: How do you feel about the judges today?

A: 今日的評審委員如何？

B: It's a lot of pressure. It will be incredible having these three judging the food. So I'm hoping they'll be a bit easier on us.

B: 壓力很大。有這三位評審委員評審食物太難得了。希望他們對我們不要太嚴厲。

A: How did you feel when you realised you had to do a dessert?

A: 你發現要做一道甜點時，有何感覺？

B: That was my worst nightmare. I don't know what an apple tart looks like, what it should taste like. I've never had one.

B: 那是我最可怕的惡夢。我不知道蘋果塔長相、味道，也從來沒吃過。

A: How are you approaching this?

A: 你如何著手？

B: I am trying to stick to this recipe. It's the best I can do.

B: 我照著食譜做。我只能這樣了。

A: What pressure is there today?	**A:** 今日壓力是什麼？
B: There's so much to do and I don't know if I'm going to have enough time to do it. That's my biggest worry.	**B:** 有太多要做的，我不確定時間夠不夠。那是我最擔憂的。
A: Have you eaten a lot of apple tarts?	**A:** 你曾吃過很多蘋果塔嗎？
B: Yes, I've had it from time to time.	**B:** 有的，我偶爾會吃一些。
A: So what do you think makes a great apple tart?	**A:** 所以如何做好吃的蘋果塔？
B: I think the pastry is very important.	**B:** 我認為派皮很重要。
A: How would you feel if you went home today?	**A:** 假如你今天回家會覺得如何？
B: Devastated.	**B:** 那就垮了。
A: How is your confidence after this morning's task?	**A:** 今早的工作完後，你的信心如何？

B: Rock bottom. One thing I don't do is give up.

B: 跌到谷底。但我絕不放棄。

本部分的實用語句都是烹飪節目中主持人及參賽者經常使用的英語。讀者習慣這些語句在與人溝通時，可充分表達個人的情緒。

- **Giving Compliments on Food 讚美食物的表達語句**

1. 我喜歡這些貝果的味道。
   I like the flavour of those bagels.
2. 這道菜看起來很棒。
   It's a great looking dish.
3. 我喜歡你的卡士達醬。很柔滑、香甜及充滿香草味。
   I love your custard. It's creamy and it's sweet and it's full of vanilla.
4. 蘋果是軟的，但派皮烤的不夠久。
   The apples are soft. But your pastry isn't cooked long enough.
5. 很美味。有來自辣椒的嗆味，糖的甜味。這些味道太神奇了。
   I think it's delicious. It's got heat from the chilli, sweetness from the sugar. Some of the flavours are magical.
6. 雞肉很棒，好吃有辣味。
   I think the chicken's great－it's nice and spicy.
7. 我喜歡檸檬雞。
   I love the lemon with the chicken.
8. 我覺得很棒。雞肉真的很嫩也溼潤。
   I thought it was fantastic. The chicken was really tender, and the moisture was still there.

9. 很軟、很辣、也有味道。調味適中。
It's soft, its spicy, full of flavour. It is well seasoned.
10. 很完美。不甜。上面也很脆。
It is just perfect. It's not too sweet. It's crunchy on the top.
11. 盤子上有些顏色是很好的。
It's nice to see some colour on your plate.
12. 菜的裝盤很漂亮。
He presented the dish beautifully.
13. 很美味。太棒了。
It tastes good. It's absolutely gorgeous.

Expressions for Excitement 表達高興的語句

1. 太美妙了。我說不出話來了。
It was absolutely brilliant. I am speechless.
2. 太美好了。我很幸運。
It has been fantastic. I feel very lucky.
3. 我沒想到有人會如此談論我做的菜。是巨大的讚美。
I never thought anybody would talk about my cooking like that. It's a huge compliment.
4. 我真的很吃驚。
I am genuinely astonished.
5. 我鬆了一口氣。
I am feeling really relieved.
6. 我真的很吃驚。完全沒想到。
I am absolutely stunned. I just wasn't expecting it.
7. 我覺得拾回了我的信心。
I feel like I'm getting my confidence back.
8. 我喜歡在專業的廚房工作，也希望能有機會再來一次。
I love to work in the professional kitchen and I hope I get the opportunity to do it again.
9. 我對做的菜很有信心。我只需確定時間足夠就行了。
I'm confident with what I'm cooking, I just have to make sure that I've got the time to cook it in.

10.很高興結束了。我喜歡參賽的每一刻。過程很辛苦，但我學了很多。

I'm glad it's over. I absolutely loved every moment of it. It's tough, but I learned a huge amount.

11.結果太好了，所有的辛苦都沒白費。

It's just such a good result, which shows the hard works really paid off.

12.我真的很震驚。無法相信。能進入賽程的一半，而且是前八名。太棒了。

I'm so shocked. I can't believe this. To get halfway through the competition and be in the top eight. It's fantastic.

- **Expressions for Disappointment 表達失望的語句**

1. 我做的不好。對我有些難。我已經亂了套了。

   I am doing quite badly. This is beyond me. I'm in a mess already.

2. 哎呀，哎呀。真是災難！

   Oh, dear, oh dear. Disaster!

3. 我很失望。我太傷心了。

   I'm disappointed. I am absolutely gutted.

4. 坦白說，我累垮了。

   To be quite honest, I am completely exhausted.

5. 這真是可怕的惡夢。

   I had an absolute nightmare.

- **Describing Cooking Methods 描述烹飪方法的語句**

1. 他們必須證明可以照著食譜做菜。

   All they have to do is to prove they can follow a recipe.

2. 我喜歡照著食譜做菜。

   When it comes to cooking, I do like to follow recipes.

3. 有一點乾。

   It's just a bit on the dry side.

4. 有一點過熟。

I think it was a bit overcooked.

5. 卡士達醬有一點稀，就酥皮甜點而言，還可以。

The custard was a bit runny, but in terms of the actual crumble, it was all right.

6. 沒有做的恰到好處。要甜一點才好。

It hasn't quite delivered. It needs to be a bit sweeter.

7. 蔬菜甜而香濃。

The vegetables are sweet and tangy.

8. 白醬調味恰好。

The white sauce is well-seasoned.

9. 淡而無味。

It's very bland.

10. 盤內別放太多食物。注意裝盤。

Don't put so much food on a plate. Have a go at presentation.

11. 肝做得非常好。馬鈴薯煎的黃又脆。

The liver is cooked really well. The potatoes are browned-up and crisp.

12. 不完美，但也不壞。

It's not perfect, but it's not bad.

13. 新鮮的食材最好。

Fresh ingredients are always better.

14. 義大利肉醬麵很好吃。肉多。

The spaghetti Bolognese is really nice. Quite meaty.

15. 甜點，我選了烤蘋果，我得說，太棒了。

For pudding, I went for the baked apple and, I have to say, it was absolutely gorgeous.

16. 很有嚼勁，很脆。

It was really chewy, crispy.

17. 開胃菜聽起來簡單，但簡單的食物往往是最好的。

The starter sounds simple, but simple foods are often the best.

18.沙拉調配得當。

It's a nice well-balanced salad.

- **Announcing the results of a competition 裁判宣布比賽結果的用語（這些句子在所有的競賽節目中都會出現）**

1. 本週的榮譽歸於約翰。

   This week the accolade goes to John.

2. 我們不得不宣布下週無法參加本節目的人了。很遺憾那位就是彼德。

   Sadly we have to announce who will not be joining us for next week's programme. I am sorry to say that the person is Peter.

3. 我們有兩項測試。記住今天你們中間有一個人要離開比賽。

   We have two tests for you. Remember one of you will leave the competition today.

4. 我們很難決定。很難評判。

   We have a difficult decision to make. It's been very hard to judge.

5. 現在我還想不出是誰。四個人中誰會先回家？

   Right now, I cannot work out who it is going to be. Which of these four is going to go home first?

7.4 Escape to the Country 移居鄉下

這個節目類型屬於購屋電視節目（Property Buying Television Programme）。2002 年起在 BBC One 每日下午 3 點播出至今。節目製作模式雖有一些改變，但基本模式維持不變。節目主持人替有需要改變環境，想從忙碌的城市搬到安靜鄉下定居的人士，尋找合適他們理想的鄉間房屋。節目中間會穿插介紹購屋地點的歷史名勝。觀賞這個節目，讓我們了解英國鄉間房屋的類型及結構，周遭環境，吸引英國人願意居住鄉間的原因。

A: What kind of country property are you looking for?

A: 你要找哪一種鄉間住宅？

B: Ideally in our new property, we'd like to have a downstairs bedroom, preferably en suite.

B: 理想而言，我們的新住宅一樓能有一間臥房，最好是套房。

C: We'd like minimum three bedrooms. One hopefully with an en suite. I'd love a utility room and a large lounge.

C: 我們希望有三間臥室。最好有一間是套房。我喜歡有雜物間和大客廳。

A: What kind of country property is going to light their fire?

A: 哪種鄉間房屋會讓他們動心？

B: We definitely want a warm, airy house. A lovely kitchen. If I could have a double range, that would be my absolute dream.

B: 我們肯定要溫暖、通風的房屋。也要很好的廚房。如果有一個雙烤箱的炊具，那絕對是我的夢想。

A: What is your wish list?

A: 你的願望清單是什麼？

B: I'd like a view of the river. That would be fabulous. I'd really love an open fire, a log burner.

B: 我希望能看到河流。那就太棒了。我也想有燒木材的壁爐。

A: What is your wish list?

A: 你的願望清單是什麼？

B: I think the three must-haves for a new property in the country would be a large, square lounge, a large kitchen with a dining area and three bedrooms and my shower cubicle, please. That would be great.

B: 新的鄉間住宅必要條件有三：寬大、方形的客廳、有用餐空間的大廚房、三間臥室及淋浴間。那將會很棒。

Q: Can you tell me your must haves for a country house?

Q: 可以告訴我你鄉間住宅的必備要件？

A1: I definitely want three bedrooms. The biggest no-no for me, although they are very pretty, is a thatched property. I am not over-keen on beams or very low ceilings, and anything that makes you feel heavy and dark.

A1: 我一定要有三間臥室。雖然有茅草屋頂的房屋漂亮，但我絕對不要。我也不特別喜歡屋樑及矮屋頂，任何沉重或陰暗的感覺。

A2: I love gardening and enjoying pruning the shrubs and landscaping it, but I don't really want a large garden in a new property. I don't want to be a slave to the garden.

A2: 我愛園藝，也喜歡修剪灌木及造園，但新屋不要大花園。我不要變成花園的奴隸。

A3: I would like a slightly bigger dining area, so that people can sit and talk to me while I am cooking.

A3: 我希望餐廳的空間大一些，這樣我做飯的時候，朋友可以坐著跟我聊天。

A: Why do you want to move to the country?

A: 你為何要搬到鄉下？

B: Our main reason for moving to the country is we both absolutely adore walking. To have a view, to have open skies, to be able to see the stars at night, and breathe fresh air.

B: 主要的原因是我們喜愛散步。有風景、寬闊的天空，夜晚可看星星、呼吸新鮮的空氣。

A: Why do you want to move to the country?

A: 你為何要搬到鄉下？

B: One of our favourite pastimes is walking, just enjoying the views and the countryside. We would like to be able to look out of the windows and to be able to walk from home.

B: 我最喜歡的休閒活動之一是散步，看鄉間風景。我們喜愛看窗外，出家門就可散步。

A: How often do you go walking?

A: 你常散步嗎？

B: When the weather's good, we'll try and go out two or three times a week.

B: 天氣好的時候，一週會散步兩三次。

A: What do you think of this area?

A: 你覺得這個地區如何？

B: It's peaceful and quiet, just what we are looking for.

B: 這裡很平和安靜，正是我們要的。

A: What do you think of the property?

A: 你認為這棟房屋如何？

B: I absolutely love the property. There isn't anything wrong with it. It's got all of the space that we need.

B: 我萬分喜歡這棟房屋。沒有任何可挑剔的。也有我們需要的足夠空間。

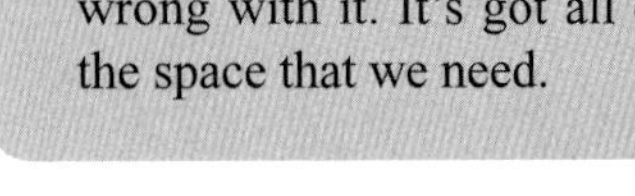

Q: Do you like this property?

Q: 你喜歡這棟房子嗎？

A1: This is the most amazing property. We could move in tomorrow. For our needs we wouldn't need to do anything to it at all. It's superlative. It's brilliant.

A1: 這棟房子太棒了。我們明天就可搬進去。我們需要的都有，不必做任何更動。超棒的。太好了。

A2: This property is perfect for both of us. I feel so comfortable. It's like home already. The kitchen is beautiful, so modern and clean and airy. The views out of the windows are spectacular. The bathroom is just perfect.

A2: 這棟房子對我們來說很完美。我感到很舒適。已經像家了。廚房很漂亮、現代、乾淨又通風。窗外的風景太壯觀了。浴室也很完美。

A3: It's got these amazingly beautiful Victorian floorboards. There is a fantastic cellar so there's a lot of storage.

A3: 房內有極美麗的維多利亞式地板。地下室極好，有很多收納空間。

A: What is the budget for this move?

A: 搬家的預算是多少？

B: Our budget for the new property is around about £275,000 - £280,000.

B: 新房屋的預算大約是 275,000 - 280,000 英鎊之間。

A: How much money is available for this move?

A: 此次搬家準備多少錢？

B: If it had everything that we wanted, and it ticked all of our boxes, it would be £450,000.

B: 假如我們要的這棟房屋都有，各項都符合我們的需求，我們就付 450,000 英鎊。

1. 天花板很低。
   The ceiling is very low.
2. 這房間一切都很好。令我驚奇萬分。
   Everything works in this room. I think it is absolutely stunning.
3. 樓上有 4 間臥室，他們認為如何？
   Upstairs there are four bedrooms, what will they make of them?
4. 這是主臥室，不大但有衛浴的套房。
   This is the master bedroom. It's not massive but it does have a very nice en suite.
5. 這是超大的穿衣間。
   Here is a gigantic walk-in wardrobe.
6. 你顯然在找辦公空間。
   You are obviously looking for office space.
7. 這棟房子是開放式空間，有 4 間臥室，車庫可改造成你要的辦公室空間，或一間樓下的臥室。
   This property has open plan living, four bedrooms, a garage that could be converted into office space, or a downstairs bedroom.

8. 我希望他們不會因為靠近繁忙的路而放棄。 真可惜這棟房子最大的缺失就是在交通繁忙的路上。

   I just hope they are not put off by the busy road. This is unfortunately the big drawback of this property. It is on a busy road.

9. 這棟房子都很好，除了這條路。

   There is nothing wrong with this house, other than the road.

10. 其他的都很好。很完美。

    Everything else is absolutely perfect. It really is perfect.

11. 這個小鎮有不同風格的房屋，有美麗茅草頂的鄉間住宅及彩繪明亮的歷史特色住宅。

    This small village has a mixture of house styles, from beautifully thatched cottages to the brightly-painted period houses.

12. 有雙層玻璃窗，可以擋噪音及保暖。

    You've got double glazed windows which is good for the noise and to keep the heat in.

13. 花園不太需要維護。房屋地點的小鎮，比我預期的小了一點。理想而言，我願意走路去商店。

    The garden is very low maintenance. The location of the property is in a smaller village than I probably hoped for. Ideally, I would like to be able to walk to the local shops.

14. 3 間臥室是大小適中的雙人房，可以招待客人。

    The three bedrooms are reasonable size doubles which can accommodate their guests.

15. 你想這房子在市面上賣多少？

    How much do you think this house is worth on the market?

16. 他們要做些妥協。

    They've got to make some compromises somewhere.

17.以 44 萬 5000 千英鎊這個價錢，這棟鄉間茅屋有他們希望的一切條件。

At £445,000, this cottage would offer them everything they're looking for.

18.天花板有點低。地點很遠。

The ceilings are quite low. The location is very remote.

19.房屋的地點很好。有很多空間。

The house is in a lovely position. There's a lot more space.

20.這棟房子有很多符合的條件。

The house ticks a lot of boxes.

1. cottage 傳統茅草房屋：這類房屋通常屋頂很低，木樑，房間也不多，但有很多英國人喜歡住這樣有特色的房屋。
2. village centre 小鎮中心：英國小鎮都會有一個 village centre 有銀行、郵局、藥店、小型超市、蔬果店、肉店，供圍繞在小鎮附近的住戶，步行就能購物、辦理日常業務。

Unit 8 Understanding Advertising

閱讀廣告

旅居英國，在衣食住行上或許會遇到一些需要自行解決的問題。讀者可在網上搜尋解決方案，但也可以利用 BT The Phone Book（英國電信局紙本電話廣告簿）。廣告簿中的分類廣告，是我們日常生活重要資訊的來源。廣告本身有提供資訊及教育大眾的功用。分類廣告對各行各業提供的服務皆有詳盡的描述，可幫助我們增進文化知識，認識新產品。閱讀一則托兒所廣告可得知入學年齡、托兒時數、教師資格等資訊；訂製門窗的廣告，則會告知顧客使用的材質及保暖隔音效果。閱讀廣告可學到大量的英語字彙，重要的關鍵字，但不需要高深的文法知識。廣告爲吸引顧客，常用雙關語及幽默的語句，讀來津津有味。

8.1 Advertisements
各類廣告

8.1a 廣告 1　HomeServe Plumbers 水管服務

Plumbing problem? 水管出問題？
We can help, call 24 hrs, fast and efficient.
我們可以幫忙，24 小時，又快又有效率。
2 hour emergency response 兩小時內緊急回應
Fixed prices 固定價格
No call out charges 上門檢查不收費
No hidden extras, prices include all parts, labour & VAT.
無隱藏額外費用，費用包括零件、人工、及附加稅。
We offer many services including: 我們提供多項服務包括：
Leaks & Bursts 漏水及水管爆裂
Tanks & Overflow 水槽及淹水
Toilets and Taps 馬桶及水龍頭
Boiler Breakdown 熱水器故障
Radiators and Pipes 暖氣及管線
Boiler Installation 安裝熱水器
Drain Jetting 疏通下水道
Gas Work 瓦斯工程
Blockages 管道堵塞
Local approved engineers 當地合格工程人員
Visit homeserve.com or call us freephone on 080024 7 999
參訪網站或撥打免費電話 080024 7 999

註 1：在英國消費都需付 VAT 即 Value Added Tax 的縮寫。消費帳單上會註明 inc vat 已含稅，excl vat 是未含稅。

註 2：call out charges 家中水管、馬桶出問題，通常找人上門檢查，不管有無修理，都需付費。因此找提供免費檢查的公司是很重要的。

註 3：hidden extras 沒有隱藏的額外費用。

註 4：英國免費電話是 0800

8.1b 廣告 2　Locksmiths 鎖匠（開鎖店）

1/2 Hour Service 半小時內上門服務
Locksmiths & Security Services 鎖匠及安全防護服務
Emergency Door Opening 緊急開門
Boarding & Burglary Repairs 安裝門窗板及防盜修理
No Call Out Charges 上門無需付費
uPVC Door and Window Specialists 安裝 uPVC 門窗專家
All Locks Supplied and Fitted 提供各種門鎖及安裝
Call Us Now Freephone 0800 035 0959 立刻撥打免費電話 0800 035 0959

註：Boarding & Burglary Repairs：Boarding 是指家中遭竊，門窗遭到破壞，需用木板暫時釘起來。Burglary Repairs 指修理竊盜破壞的事物。

8.1c 廣告 3　Gormans Fish and Chips Gormans 炸魚薯條店

Our Take Out Menu 外帶菜單

Taking out? We serve the best dish and the perfect portion. We're sure you'll want to experience Gormans again and again so we'll make it fab first time round. Pop in our Great British Fish & Chips.

外帶嗎？我們提供最好的菜及完美的分量。我們肯定您們願意一次次體驗 Gormans，也會讓菜色像第一次一樣的「美好」。請來光顧我們偉大的英國炸魚薯條店。

Visit your local Gormans to taste the difference and discover for yourself the delights of our Great British fish &chips. Find us on facebook, follow us on twitter or find our take away menu and specials at www.lovegormans. co.uk

到你常光顧的 Gormans 店，品嘗並發現我們偉大的英國炸魚和薯條。你可在臉書找到我們，也可以上我們的 twitter 也可以在 www.lovegormans.co.uk 找到我們的外帶菜單及特色菜。

註 1：fab 是 fabulous（極好的或美好的）一字的縮寫。

註 2：Fish and Chips 炸魚和薯條就像我們的便當，是英國非常普遍的速食。薯條比細細的 French Fries 要大條厚實。買了一份 fish and chips 店員通常會問：Salt and vinegar?（要加鹽跟醋嗎？）請人喝茶也要問：Milk and Sugar? 到速食店如麥當勞，點完餐，服務員會問：To eat here or take away?

8.1d 廣告 4　Nursery 托兒所

Maple Lodge Nursery 托兒所
OFSTED registered OFSTED 註冊合格
Learning through play since 1987 自 1987 年起 玩樂中學習
Your child is our priority 您的孩子是我們的優先考慮
Welcoming, warm and friendly environment with incredibly attentive staff with excellent facilities for all ages.
感受歡迎、溫暖、友善的環境，極為專注的員工及適合各種年紀的優質設備。
Staff go out of their way to accommodate individual needs. Children are happy to attend and develop into confident secure individuals.
員工不怕麻煩照顧每個人的需求。孩童樂意上學並成長為有自信有安全感的人。
Open 52 weeks 營業 52 週
Flexible hours 時間有彈性
Full time concessions 全日班有優惠
Safe and friendly environment 友善安全的環境
Excellent facilities 完善的設備
Fully trained and qualified staff 受過完整培訓合格的員工
All religions & diets 無宗教及飲食限制
6 weeks to school age 從出生六週到學齡
CCTV monitored 閉路電視監控
Vouchers accepted 接受禮券
Nursery Grant sessions for children 3+ 3 歲以上提供托兒所助學金課程
Caring for children as individuals 將孩童視為獨立個體照顧

註 1：OFSTED 是 Office for Standards in Education, Children's Services and Skills 的簡稱，是負責監督全英國各級學校的教育品質及提升教育水準的重要機構。任何學校得到此機構的認可，就是品質保證。

註 2：培養人格的自信心、安全感是英國教育很重要的目標之一。

註 3：有的學校僅收特定宗教信仰（如回教、天主教、英國國教）的學生。這所托兒所沒有宗教信仰的限制也沒有飲食限制（如回教人士不吃豬肉）。

8.1e 廣告 5　Garage Services 汽車維修廠

Vehicle Servicing, Repairs & Mot's 汽車保養、維修及汽車檢測
Repairs to All Makes and Models 修理各種汽車廠牌及類型
Mechanical Repairs 機械修理
Servicing Specialists 保養行家
Bosch Diagnostics Bosch 汽車檢測設備
Exhausts & Tyres 排氣管及輪胎
MOT Testing 交通部汽車檢測
Timing Belts 時規皮帶
MOT 檢測項目包括：
Vehicle Identification Number 汽車認證編號
Registration Plate Lights 牌照燈
Steering and Suspension 方向盤及懸吊系統
Wipers and Washer Bottle 雨刷及清洗瓶
Windscreen 擋風玻璃
Horn 喇叭
Seatbelts 安全帶
Seats 座位
Fuel System 燃料系統
Emission 廢氣排放
Bodywork 車身
Doors and Mirrors 車門及後照鏡
Wheels and Tyres 車輪及輪胎
Brakes 剎車

註：英國交通部（The Ministry of Transport）規定所有汽車開了 3 年後，都需通過交通部檢測項目 MOT（The Ministry of Transport Test）才可繼續使用。一般汽車修理廠可向交通部申請做 MOT 檢測服務，交通部核准後，始可發給 MOT 檢測合格證書。汽車駕駛人每年通過檢測後，才可上路。檢測不過的項目，需修理後再次檢測，直到合格爲止。檢查項目都是以路駕安全爲原則，故收費不高，約 50 英鎊。

8.1f 廣告 6　Boiler Rescue from British Gas 來自大英瓦斯的鍋爐救援

One-off emergency boiler repair 一次解決緊急鍋爐修理

Every 15 seconds a boiler breaks down in the UK, but don't worry－your local British Gas engineer is here to help.

英國每 15 秒鐘就有一個鍋爐故障，但不用擔心，你當地的大英瓦斯工程人員會幫忙。

A competitive fixed price including parts and labour, so you'll know exactly how much you have to pay.

有競爭力的固定價格，包括零件與人工，這樣你會知道要付的價錢。

A boiler diagnostic and safety check to quickly identify the problem.

診斷鍋爐及安全檢查，快速檢出問題。

We hope this gives you some peace of mind when it comes to looking after your home and fingers crossed, you won't need us any time soon.

由我們來照顧您的家，讓您安心，同時祈求好運，近期內您不再需要我們。

Get an instant quote 可立即估價

You don't have to wait until you are in a breakdown situation to call us. We can cover your boiler and central heating system as well as your plumbing, drains and fixed electrics－helping you to avoid the unexpected expense of repair bills.

您不需要等到鍋爐故障才打電話。我們可以提供保險，保固您的鍋爐、中央暖氣系統、水管、下水道、固定家用電器，助你免除額外的修理費用。

註 1：British Gas 是英國最大的瓦斯公司，boiler 鍋爐或熱水器是英國家庭中最重要的設備。冬天屋中的暖氣（central heating）及熱水都靠它，一般英國人最擔心的就是鍋爐故障。因此廣告中特別強調 British Gas 會帶給客戶安心（peace of mind）。

註 2：英國居住萬事都要買保險。住屋保險、汽車險、家中鍋爐、電器等也需要保險。因此找優良品牌的保險公司投保，平時付保險費，出了問題費用由保險公司支付。

8.1g 廣告 7 PrimeGas Services (www.primegasservices.co.uk) PrimeGas 檢修服務

Central Heating Engineers 中央暖氣工程
Full Systems Installed & Upgrades 整體系統安裝及升級
Combi & Condensing Boilers 合併式及凝結式鍋爐
Replacement Radiators & Pipework 更換暖氣及管線
All Plumbing & Heating Work Undertaken 承包所有水道及暖氣工程
Burst Pipes 爆管工程
Complete Installations and Repairs 全面安裝及修理
- 95% of work (installations) Done in 1 Day
  95% 的工程（安裝）可在一天內完成
- Fully Insured and Guaranteed 保全險並保修
- Safe and Secure 安全可靠
- Gas Leak Repairs & Reconnection 修理瓦斯漏氣及重接
- Boilers Installation & Repairs 鍋爐安裝及修理
- Gas Safety Checks 瓦斯安全檢查
- Fit Gas Cookers & Fires 安裝瓦斯爐及壁爐
- Gas Pipework 瓦斯管線工程
10% Discount for Senior Citizens 年長者 9 折優待
Free friendly advice and estimates 免費友善的建議及估價

8.1h 廣告 8 HomeCare Removals and Storage HomeCare 搬家及貯藏保管

Why Choose HomeCare 爲何選擇 HomeCare
Household & Business Removals 家庭及公司搬家
Piano Movers 搬鋼琴
Antique Movers 搬古董
Packing / Un-packing Service 打包 / 拆包服務
Senior Citizen Discount 年長者優惠
Contract Work Undertaken 接受承包業務
Local－National－International 當地—國內—國際
Furniture Wraps 包裹家具
Carpet Protectors 地毯保護服務

Cheerful, Uniformed Staff 快樂穿制服的員工
Fully Insured Service 投保全險服務
Indoor Heated Storage 溫室貯藏
House Clearances 清空房屋
Licensed Rubbish Removals 持有垃圾搬運執照
Packing Materials Available 提供包裝材料
100% Reliable Services 百分百可靠服務

註 1：這是搬家公司的廣告所提供的服務項目。很多英國人家中有祖先留下來的古董，搬家公司會特別小心包裝搬運，因此搬運費也會很貴。搬家公司需要投保全險（fully insured），萬一出了問題，可由保險公司賠償。

註 2：在英國買房賣房，有時無法按時搬進搬出，需找搬家公司提供貯藏空間（Storage），按租用時間長短計費。無法按時搬到新家時，只能將家當存放在租用的貯藏櫃，人則住到親朋好友家，或住旅館。等對方房屋清空後，擇日再搬。如此看來，搬家有很多額外花費。

8.1i 廣告 9　Everest Windows and Doors Everest 門窗訂製

Making more of your environment 充分利用你的環境
New! Our most energy efficient windows 新！我們最節省能源的窗戶
- Widest range of window and door styles in uPVC, timber and aluminium
  各種樣式的 uPVC，木材、鋁製的窗門
- Tailor-made & virtually maintenance free 專門訂製及幾乎無需保養
- Retain 2 times more heat than ordinary double glazing and 4 times more than ordinary single glazing
  比一般雙層玻璃窗可保暖兩倍以上，比一般單層玻璃窗四倍以上
- 10 year, 30 year + lifetime guarantees 10 年、30 年、終生保固

Warm, quiet, secure, draught-free - you can't beat Everest Windows and Doors
提供溫暖、安靜、安全、不透風的門窗，沒有比的上 Everest Windows and Doors

8.1j 廣告 10　Alex PC Repairs Alex 電腦維修

No fix - No fee 修不好一不收費
Hardware and software 硬體和軟體
PC too slow? 電腦太慢？
Internet problems 網路問題
Virus problems 病毒問題
Laptop screens 筆記電腦顯示器
Free call out 上門免收費
Microsoft qualified engineer 微軟合格工程師

8.1k 廣告 11　Q Hair Q 髮廊

Providing Excellence in Hairdressing and Hair Care for over 17 years. 十七年來提供優質的美髮、護髮服務。
Blow Dry £12.00 吹 12.00 英鎊
Cut & Blow Dry £19.50 剪和吹 19.50 英鎊
Gent's Cut & Blow Dry £13.50 男士剪吹 13.50 英鎊
Full Head Colour £40 整頭染 40 英鎊
1/2 Head of Hi Lites £52.50 半頭挑染 52.50 英鎊
Full Head Hi Lites £62.50 整頭挑染 62.50 英鎊
Perms Starting from £ 45.00 燙髮 45.00 英鎊起

註：這是一般英國髮廊所提供的美髮項目。高級髮廊如 Toni&Guy 則會依照：Stylist（設計師）、Senior Stylist（資深造型設計師）、Top International Stylist（國際頂級造型設計師）等級收費。

8.2 Advertising Vouchers 廣告折價券

廣告的目的是鼓勵並說服顧客消費，跟我們生活息息相關的廣告，超市折價券廣告最為普遍。此類折價券，為了立刻達到吸引顧客的注意，折扣用醒目的大字體，而使用此券的重要信息及使用條件，則用小字體。因此在英國常會聽到一句話：Always look at the small prints.（永遠都要讀小字體）。本節提供的廣告樣本，旨在說明看小字的重要性。

8.2a £15 off 15 英鎊優惠券

When you spend £75 or more on your first online grocery shop from Sainsburys.co.uk, enter this 12 digit voucher code when you checkout online. 47QMF DF GL NTM

當你第一次在 Sainsburys.co.uk 網購 75 英鎊以上的物品時，可折價 15 英鎊。結帳時輸入消費券上 12 位數字代碼 47QMF DF GL NTM。

註：優惠 15 英鎊用醒目的大字體，吸引顧客，而使用這張折價券必須先消費 75 英鎊則用小字體。因此使用折價券消費時，一定要先看說明或使用條件。

8.2b Save £10 on your first £50 Sainsbury's online grocery shop 首次在 Sainsbury 的食品網店購物，花 50 英鎊立減 10 英鎊。

Plus free mid-week delivery if you spend over £100 消費 100 英鎊以上可享免費平日送貨。

註 1：此張優惠券的條件是必須先花 50 英鎊才可得 10 英鎊的優惠；花 100 英鎊只能平日免費送貨，不包括週五、六、日。

註 2：Sainsburys 是英國四大超市之一（UK Big Four supermarkets），其他三家是 Tesco (http://www.tesco.com/), Asda (http://www.asda.com/), Morrison (http://www.morrisons.co.uk/)。另有超市不是「四大」，但品質特好價位較高：Marks and Spencer（http://www.marksandspencer.com/）及 Waitrose（http://www.waitrose.com/）。現在流行網購（online shopping），在此將四大

超市的網址提供給讀者。網路科技的普及，使我們秀才不出門，可知天下事。讀者也可以上網虛擬網購一下，增加日常生活的英語字彙，同時也可參考比較各大超市的產品價格。

8.2c Great City Attractions 城市吸睛景點

15% online discount 網購享 15% 折扣
Valid until 1st January 2016 有效日至 2016 年一月一日
Not to be used in conjunction with any other offer.
不可與其他的優惠同時使用。
This voucher must be handed to the cashier to receive discount.
將此折價券給售票員以取得折扣。
Times and availability may change due to maintenance, weather or other operational reasons.
因維修、氣候及其他操作因素，得以改變使用時間及有效性。
註：使用優惠券要先看有效期限（valid until）及使用限制。

1. 照片印表機半價。原價 120 英鎊，現 60 英鎊。
   Photo printer half price. Normal price: £120, now £60!
2. 購買 50 英鎊義大利酒，送一個免費披薩。
   Spend £50 on Italian wine and get a free pizza.
3. 飛都柏林，票價 20 英鎊起。
   Fly to Dublin, fares from £20.
4. 不出門一小時就能賺 30 英鎊。
   Earn £30 an hour in your own home.
5. 買彩券，中百萬英鎊！
   Play the Lottery and win £1,000,000!
6. 網上付電費，我們立減 2%。
   Pay for your electricity online and we'll take 2% off.

7. 想僱一位值得花錢的建築工人：讀我們的資料簡介就好，不用花一分錢。

   How to get your money's worth when hiring a builder: read our factsheet and it won't cost you a penny.

8. 搭飛機旅行：不要被敲——找 travel.co.uk.。

   Air travel: don't get ripped off – come to travel.co.uk.

9. 你已負債而憂心了？我們可幫忙。

   You've run up a debt and are worried about it? We can help.

10. 同學們：不要負債過日子。買學生理財雜誌。

    Students: keep your head above the water! Buy Student Finance Magazine.

11. 有欠債難題？假如債務毀了你的人生，立刻撥打我們的電話。

    Debt Problems? If debt is destroying your life then call us now.

12. 出國別缺錢：帶旅行支票。

    Don't run out of money abroad: take Traveller's cheques.

13. 我們的保險包括牙齒治療。

    Our insurance will cover the cost of dental work.

14. 童話式交易——20Mb 寬頻、Sky 有線電視及撥打電話一三項 20 英鎊以內——永遠快樂。

    A Fairytale Deal – Up to 20 Mb broadband, SkyTV and calls – All 3 for under £20 – Happily Ever After.

15. 保持冷靜，假如夏日汽車故障，參加 AA 故障搶修，只要 35 英鎊。

    Stay cool if you break down this summer, join the AA from just £35.

16. 省錢省能源。

    Save money. Save energy.

17. 只有在你的 M&S。

    Only at your M&S.

18.我們獨自測試了我們的學生制服。洗過 30 次後，就耐用、顏色鮮度及外觀，和其他商業街的六家競爭者比較，我們是最上等的。所以艱難的工作我們做，您的小孩可以盡情的玩。

We have independently tested our uniforms against six other high street competitors, and ours came top of the class for durability, colour retention and appearance over 30 washes. So now we've done all the hard work, your kids can do all the hard play.

註 1：Marks and Spencer：簡稱 M&S 英國極受大眾歡迎的品牌百貨公司。

註 2：high street：英國大小城鎮都有一條 high street（商店街），重要的商店及百貨公司都集中在這個商業區，方便顧客逛街購物。

Appendixes

附錄

1. 說英語需要有「美國口音」？
2. 英式英語 vs. 美式英語：以《哈利波特與魔法石》小說為例（British English vs. American English: *Harry Potter and the Philosopher's Stone*）
3. 口語練習最好的方法：跟念（Shadow Reading）
4. 情境英語對話的迷思
5. Tea, Dinner, Supper 哪一餐？
6. The X Factor 「X」字母的含意

1. 說英語需要有「美國口音」？

在英國曼徹斯特大學（The University of Manchester）修英國文學博士學位期間，重新認識並思考一些英語學習的問題。第一次和論文指導老師見面時，他很客氣也有一點不好意思地問：「爲何你說英語有美國口音？」我很訝異他的問題，我們在臺灣學英語不是應該有個美國腔才好嗎？當時只回答說很多教英語的老師都是美國人，他沒說話。後來我發現，遇到的英國人都會問同樣的問題，好像我說英語有美國腔是非常奇怪的事。

我開始思考「口音」的問題，同時參加了許多英語教學研討會，觀摩英國語言老師的教學方法。我特別注意這些英語教學專家處理外國學生口音的態度。我發現他們的看法是：老師的教學目標應是訓練學生的表達能力，能夠正確地使用英語，所以根本不會浪費時間要學生模仿母語人士說話。換言之，正港臺灣人說英語帶有臺灣口音，是一件非常自然而且也有政治正當性（politically correct）。因此說國語有口音，說英語也有口音，也就是說，只要開口說話，就無法免除口音（accent-free）。我也觀察到歐洲人說英語都有自己的腔調；荷蘭人的英語，說的流利、句子文法正確、用字優雅，但都帶有濃厚的荷蘭口音。因此口音不是「病」，不需要「治療」。口音不會影響英語能力檢定測驗的成績，也不會用來判斷英語程度的高下。

得到英國文學博士回國再教英語時，我開始注意「美國口音」對學生學習的影響。我問學生爲何不願意大聲念英語，答案都是因爲自己發音不好，也就是說沒有美國腔。原來說英語要有美國腔這個大錯特錯的觀念，引起這麼嚴重的焦慮。我告訴學生學英語要學正確的英語，不追求說英語要像母語人士 ，更不需要美國口音。當學生從美國腔的迷思解脫出來，他們對自己說的英語有了信心，口語進步飛快。

另一方面，說英語要有美國腔的焦慮對英語學習產生許多嚴重的障礙。人人都希望能說一口流利的美語，當無法開口表達己見時，便怪罪缺少與美籍母語人士交談的機會，以及臺灣不是一個說英語的美國環境。這些因素使無法開口說英語合理化，找到一個聽起來相當合理的藉口，卻使學習者永遠停留在依賴老師（特別是美籍母語人士）的階段。久而久之，人人都在等待名師指點，反而忽略了語言學習最基本的認知：那就是語言學習需持之以恆及長久不斷的努力。

不追求說英語要像母語人士，放棄說英語要有美國口音，要說流利的英語一點也不困難。每天大聲朗讀英語，隨時聽英語，替自己創造一個英語環境，相信你的英語一定會有驚人的進步。

2. 英式英語 vs. 美式英語：以《哈利波特與魔法石》小說為例（British English vs. American English: *Harry Potter and the Philosopher's Stone*）

讀者也許有興趣知道為何 J. K. Rowling 的第一本小說有兩個不同的書名？1997 年英國出版的書名是 *Harry Potter and the Philosopher's Stone*（中文譯名應是《哈利波特與點金石》）。作者羅琳直接用了煉金術理論中最重要的關鍵字「點金石」（Philosopher's Stone），清楚指出這是一本與煉金術相關的小說。「點金石」有特異功能，能點鐵成金，讓人致富並長生不老。哈利波特的父母都是正派的煉金術士，哈利波特是煉金術士之子，他的人生使命就是保護這個珍貴的「點金石」，以免落入壞人之手。

1999 年美國發行的版本及電影將書名改為 *Harry Potter and the Sorcerer's Stone*《哈利波特與神祕的魔法石》，羅琳也許考慮到美國讀者無法了解「點金石」這個複雜的專有名詞，因此改為較通俗易懂的「魔法石」，但也喪失了小說與煉金術深層的關聯。

這兩個版本除了書名不同，內文也將英國版的英式英語詞彙及拼字，更改為美式英語的用法。茲從兩個版本中挑出一些常用的詞彙供讀者參考。有興趣的讀者可以逛逛內容豐富的波特網站：*Harry Potter and the Philosopher's Stone* (http://www.hp-lexicon.org/about/books/ps/differences-ps.html)。

British English（英國版）	American English（美國版）
Philosopher's Stone 點金石	Sorcerer's Stone
mum 媽媽	mom
packet of crisps 一包薯條	bag of chips
holidaying 度假	vacationing
queuing 排隊	lining up
bins 垃圾桶	trash cans

cinema 電影	movies
ice lolly 冰棒	ice pop
post 郵件	mail
jumper 套頭毛衣	sweater
car park 停車場	parking lot
motorway 高速公路	highway
comprehensive 公立學校	public school
trolley 手推車	cart
trainers 運動鞋	sneakers
football 足球	soccer
sweets 糖果	candy
Happy Christmas 聖誕快樂	Merry Christmas
change rooms 更衣室	locker room

英式與美式英語拼字的差異並不多，茲舉例如下：

British English（簡稱 BrE）	American English（簡稱 AmE）
organise 組織	organize
programme 節目	program
dialogue 對話	dialog
analyse 分析	analyze
encyclopaedia 百科全書	encyclopedia
colour 顏色	color
honour 榮譽	honor
aeroplane 飛機	airplane
theatre 劇院	theater

欲了解英式與美式英語發音上的差別，線上字典如《劍橋英語字典》*Cambridge Dictionary*（http://dictionary.cambridge.org/dictionary/british/）、《牛津英語字典》*Oxford Learner's Dictionary*（http://www.oxfordlearnersdictionaries.com/）皆提供英式及美式發音的聲音檔，因此花時間學音標已經是老舊的英語學習方法了。茲舉幾個有代表性的單字，請讀者上這兩部字典的網站，很容易聽出這些字發音的不同。

advertisement *noun* [C] UK /ədˈvɜː.tɪs.mənt/ US /ˈæd.vɝː.taɪz.mənt/	garage *noun* UK /ˈgær.ɑːʒ/ /-ɪdʒ/ US /gəˈrɑːʒ/
tomato *noun* [C or U] UK /təˈmɑː.təʊ/ US /-ˈmeɪ.t̬oʊ/ (PLURAL **tomatoes**)	schedule *noun* [C] UK /ˈʃed.juːl/ US /ˈsked-/
vase *noun* [C] UK /vɑːz/ US /veɪs/	class *noun* UK /klɑːs/ US /klæs/

英式英語句子的語調節奏、字的輕重音，非常清楚，而英語詩歌的節奏、抑揚頓挫與押韻，是幫助我們說準確流利英語的最佳材料。讀者有興趣多聽一些英式英語詩歌朗讀，可進入臺大圖書館數位學習網，筆者主講的「英語聽力訓練課程」（http://mediahive.lib.ntu.edu.tw/website/chou/chou.htm），其中有一節詳細說明詩歌朗讀的目標與方法。讀者可選擇自己喜愛的詩歌、童話故事、小說名著，聆聽名家朗讀，並大聲跟念（Shadow Reading）。若能持之以恆，您的英語自然會說的清楚、流利、有節奏感！

3. 口語練習最好的方法：跟念（Shadow Reading）

Shadow Reading 兩字的意思是「影子朗讀」，學習者像影子，跟著老師或有聲文章朗讀。讀者皆知，英語是一個節奏（Rhythm）的語言，念起來有輕、重音、有速度（Tempo）。也就是說，一句話念起來不是以單字爲單位，而是以字組爲單位，說話的速度則是快快慢慢。跟念是一種多元化的口語練習，因爲學習者必須跟著聽到的英語朗讀，因此不但可學到單字的正確發音，更可掌握句子中字的輕重音（Stress）、連音（Linking Words）、字組（Thought Groups）、以及句子整體的語調（Intonation）。多多跟念，持之以恆，可使英語說的流利自然，是提升口語能力的最佳方法。

爲說明跟念的好處，試舉一簡單例句分析：This is the house that Jack built.

這句話，當我們看著文字念的時候，字都是一樣大，念不出輕重快慢，也看不出句子中的停頓。但依據英語的節奏，句子中的名詞、動詞、形容詞、副詞要念重，才能將意思表達清楚。因此這句話念起來應該是：

This is the **house** that / **Jack built.**

此處名詞、動詞用大的黑體字標示，代表重音，要念重、念慢；小的字要念輕、念快，有些字要黏在一起念。「/」這個符號代表「字組」（Thought Group/Sense Group）及「停頓」（Pause）。因此在大聲跟念時，我們自然就會隨著聽到的聲音，將字組合在一起，意識到英語的節奏。不僅如此，跟念也會提醒我們經常會遺漏的字尾（word ending）：That sounds great. I have two pictures. 動詞後的 s 及名詞的多數，漏掉字尾造成文法錯誤。另外，我們也會發現英語有很多連音：They plan to rob us. rob us（搶我們）兩字念快了聽起來就像 bus（公車），但必須要連起來念，才會說的自然流利。這些都需要讀者不斷嘗試，用耳朵仔細聽，用嘴巴大聲念。

通常與人溝通時，讀者可能會發現，每一個字都說清楚了，爲何對方聽不懂。有一個最重要的關鍵，那就是忽略了構成句子節奏的「字組」（Thought Group）與停頓（Pause）。若是沒有將句子分成有意義的小段或字組，則無法清楚表達意義；適當的停頓，是爲了給聽話者思考的時間。茲舉幾個例句說明：

(1) Did you kill the chicken in the kitchen? 這句話斷句的地方 Did you kill 及 Did you kill the chicken 會造成句意的不同。
   (a) Did you kill / the chicken in the kitchen? 你殺了廚房裡的雞嗎？
   (b) Did you kill the chicken / in the kitchen? 你在廚房殺雞嗎？

(2) Lisa said, 'My dog is intelligent.'
   (a) Lisa said, / 'My dog is intelligent.' 麗莎說：「我的狗很聰明。」
   (b) 'Lisa, ' / said my dog, / 'is intelligent. ' 將 said my dog 念成一組，就變成狗說麗莎很聰明。

(3) Woman, without her man, is a beast.
   (a) Woman, / without her man, / is a beast. 將 without her man 念成一個字組，意思是：「女人，沒有她的男人，是野獸。」
   (b) Woman, without her, / man is a beast. 如果將 Woman, without her 念成一組，意義就剛好相反：「女人，沒有她，男人是野獸。」

這幾個例子足以說 Thought Groups 的重要性；而句子中適當的停頓，展示出讀者良好的英語節奏感及說英語的高度自信。

讀者一定會問：過去學英語跟著老師念，現在如何取得跟念的資源自學？個人認爲英國廣播公司（British Broadcasting Corporation BBC）的 Learning English「學習英語」網站（http://www.bbc.co.uk/learningenglish），是一個值得讀者終身使用的免費網路資源。Learning English 網站內容包羅萬象，最可貴的是網站上的資訊，時時刻刻都在更新，上線的讀者隨時都與世界接軌。首頁分兩大類：課程（Courses）及專題（Features）。課程內容有字彙、文法講解及各種有趣的文法習題。豐富的專題討論則有：「我們說的英語」（The English We Speak）、「新聞英語單詞」（Words in the News）、「六分鐘英語」（6 Minute English）、發音（Pronunciation）、戲劇（Drama）、新聞報導（News Report）。這些資料只要有聲音檔及文字檔都適合用來做跟念練習。

一般來說，Learning English 的節目主持人說的英語多爲字正腔圓的 RP（Received Pronunciation），值得讀者依據個人的喜好，選擇跟念的材料。我會推薦大家使用每週更新的 Words in the News。節目主持人的英語說的非常清楚，容易跟念，文章很短但知識很新，因此學到的新單詞也是實用的。PDF 文字檔及 MP3 聲音檔都可下載到手機中，隨時聽、念。跟念的步驟如下：(1) 點開聲音檔對照文字跟念；(2) 念不順單詞或句子，可以單獨反覆練習；(3) 跟念數次跟上速度後，將聲音檔聲音關小，自己朗讀聲音增大。(4) 若能不看文字，朗讀速度與聲音檔同步，那就表示這段學習成功了。讀者若能利用手機的錄音功能，每天錄一段，持之以恆，相信很快就會發現您的口語進步神速！

有人擔心跟念英式英語，會導致自己的英語說的不英、不美，這個憂慮大可不必。跟念的目標不是模仿母語人士的口音，也不是在鍛鍊什麼口音。重要的目的是讓自己說準確的英語：正確的單字發音、字有輕重、句子有節奏。有興趣終身學習英語的讀者，可充分利用豐富的 BBC Learning English 網站，選取個人有興趣的英語資料，下載到手機中，給自己創造一個聽、說、讀、寫隨身攜帶的英語學習環境。這種學習方法就是目前最流行的「移動學習」（Mobile Learning）。

語言學習是非常個人的，沒有一個標準或對錯的學習模式。本文所提供的跟念口語學習方式是開口說英語的出發點，久而久之，讀者都會找到適合自己學習的方式，變成一個獨立自主的終身學習者。一旦英語學習從課堂狹隘的空間中解放出來，擺脫對母語人士或老師的依賴，英語能力就會突飛猛進！

4. 情境英語對話的迷思

讀者一定都很熟悉英語課本中必備的「情境對話」：一個場景、數句簡短對話。學習者扮演情境中的角色（role play），模擬對話。此種被動式的練習，並不能讓學習者主動思考如何發問，並延伸談話的內容。因此問題的性質關係到溝通的順暢。英語問題（句）可分兩種類型：Closed-ended Questions（封閉式問題）及 Open-ended questions（開放式問題）。Closed-ended Questions 多以 Are...? Will...? Is...? Would...? Do...? Have...? 開始：

Are you happy?（你快樂嗎？）Yes, I am.

Do you like films?（你喜歡看電影嗎？）Yes, I do.

Is English your favourite subject?（英語是你喜歡的科目嗎？）No, it isn't.

Would you like a cup of tea?（要喝茶嗎？）Yes, please.

Do you like to walk in the rain?（你喜歡在雨中散步嗎？）No, I don't.

這些問句只要回答 yes, no 即可，答話的人沒有發揮的餘地；問話的人能得到的信息也有限，因此談話立刻結束。這也是為何讀者所認識的「情境對話」多以四、或六句為主。

開放式的問題多以 How...? When...? Where...? What...? Which...? Why...? Who...? 開始：

What do you like doing in your spare time?（空閒愛做什麼？）

How do you describe yourself?（你如何描寫自己？）

Who is your hero?（誰是你的英雄？）

Why do you want to go to the UK?（為何要去英國？）

此類問題不能簡單的用「是、否」回答，必須要給予詳細的說明，因此可以延伸談話的內容。社交場合、新朋友、各種情況的面談，多使用開放式問題。學習如何發問「開放式問題」，如何回答這類問題，才能真正達到用英語與人溝通的目的。

為讓讀者充分了解「開放式問題」的重要性，並多多練習延伸對話，本書所提供的情境對話有長有短，可以情境對話，也是很好的閱讀材料，一舉數得。另外，讀者想必了解，旅居英國，與人面對面對話的機會並不多，因此花時間多聽、多讀，比與人對話來的更重要。

5. Tea, Dinner, Supper 哪一餐？

讀者都認識這三個與飲食相關的字眼，但也許沒有想到，tea, dinner, supper 所指的一日三餐，依據說話人的身分、社會背景、地域，有不同的含意。

當英國人說：Come before tea time. 或 See you after tea. 這裡的 tea 是指「茶」還是「晚餐」？應該幾點鐘見面？若是英國友人跟你說： Come around for dinner. 他是請你吃中餐還是晚餐？幾點鐘吃？那麼 supper 指的是哪一餐？

英國人從南到北，不管身分、階級，早餐都稱 breakfast，由 break + fast 兩個字組成，意思是打破前一晚的飢餓，就是一天的第一餐。早餐飲料有果汁、茶、咖啡，土司麵包、麥片、三明治、或 fry up（「煎物」：包括煎蛋、煎香腸、煎培根、煎薯餅）。因爲都是用煎的，就統稱爲 fry up。英國的 B&B（Bed and Breakfast）提供的早餐都是 fry up，客人吃一個豐富的早餐，就可以出門旅遊了。

至於 dinner 與 tea 是午餐還是晚餐，則看說話人的社會背景。居住在英國北方的中下層階級（lower middle class）及勞工階級人士（working class），傳統稱午餐（dinner）（afternoon meal）；與 dinner 相關的字有：dinner time 午餐時間（12 - 1 pm），school dinner 指中小學學校供應的午餐，dinner ladies 是爲學生料理中餐的阿姨，dinner money 是午餐費。

tea 是晚餐（evening meal），tea time 不是喝茶時間，是晚餐時間，約五、六點鐘。對英國北方勞工階級人士來說，這是一天最重要的一頓飯。當人說 Come before tea time. 是指四點鐘左右；See you after tea. 指六點左右。而 supper（pre-bed snack）則是指晚上上床之前吃的小點，如一杯可可、牛奶、餅乾、一片土司。來自北方的勞工階級人士的一日三餐是：breakfast, dinner, tea。

英國南方的上流社會人士（upper social classes）稱午餐爲 lunch（midday meal）或 luncheon，而 dinner 是指約七點鐘吃的正式晚餐（the evening meal）。supper 則是在廚房或電視機前吃的簡餐。kitchen supper 或 country supper 指跟朋友一起吃的便餐，喝點酒，配簡單的小菜、起司（cheese）、水果。英國上流社會人士的一日三餐依序是：breakfast, lunch, dinner, supper。而 tea 是指下午茶（afternoon tea），通常在花園或家中沙發旁的茶几進行。搭配喝茶的點心有：夾有黃瓜、鮪魚的三明治、各種蛋糕、司康餅（scones）。

dinner, tea, supper 因階級及地域所造成用法的差異，難免會產生一些溝通誤會。當南方人士說：Come for dinner. 北方人會以爲是請吃中飯。但這種差異，隨著時間逐漸減少，有時 dinner / lunch 兩字互換使用，白天中餐是 dinner，晚餐就是 tea；中餐是 lunch，那麼晚餐就是 dinner。

6. The X Factor 「X」字母的含意

The X Factor 原意是指某人有難以形容但又極爲關鍵性的特質或未知數。*The X Factor* 也是英國商業電視台 ITV 製作的才藝競賽節目名稱。但 x 字母另有含意。

網路時代旅居英國的讀者，在處理日常生活的事務上，用英語寫 email 及發短訊，恐怕比與人面對面溝通的機會來的多。因此了解一點英國人的書信文化，有利於書面溝通，並可避免不必要的誤會。

讀者都熟悉正式的英語書信基本格式：以 Dear 開頭；書信對象若是不熟悉的人，則以 Yours sincerely, Yours faithfully, 結尾，親近的人則用 Yours truly。隨著 email 電子郵件快速傳遞信件的性質，傳統的書信形式顯的非常累贅。電子郵件不再用正式的書信格式：Dear 用 Hi 代替，結尾多用 Best Wishes 或 Warm Regards。也有愈來愈多的人（特別是用手機的年輕人），省略了文字，信尾屬名後僅用 x 字母或數個 xxx 如 Susan x。

爲何用 x 字母？也許因爲 x 字母發音 [ks] 與 kiss 接近，確切的由來不可考。英國人用 x 代表 kiss（空氣傳送的親吻），表達熱情，但僅限親朋好友、關係親密的人士之間。傳統紙本的書信中，寫信的人清楚知道與讀信對象的關係，因此在信尾附上很多 xxx 表示給對方很多親吻及傳達說不盡的親密情感。英國首相邱吉爾的信中曾出現這樣的句子：

Please excuse bad writing as I am in an awful hurry. (Many kisses.) xxx WSC

請原諒寫的不周，因過忙碌（很多親吻）xxx WSC 上

現今 email 及簡訊的普及，使用 x 的現象愈來愈普遍，原來 x 的特殊意義及代表 kiss 的含意也就逐漸消除了。寄信人往往忘了與收信人的關係，不自覺在信尾附上幾個 xxx ，如此隨意使用 x 會不會引起誤會？很多時候，辦公室老闆與員工之間的 email 來往，因爲信尾多了一個 x 讓收信人誤以爲對方向其示好，引來一段意外的「辦公室情事」。也有學生給老師的 email 不小心（或有意）加了 x 使老師以爲學生在示愛。電子版的 x，就像男女之間有意無意的身體碰觸，會引發意想不到的後果，不可不小心使用。

那麼如何使用 x 才不會引起誤會呢？閨蜜之間用 x 表達熱絡的情感，是很恰當的。男女之間用 x 代表 kiss 則要仔細思考與對方的關係，以免產生誤解。必須要給 kiss 的話，最多三個 xxx 也就足夠了。

國家圖書館出版品預行編目資料

開口就會英國長住用語 / 周樹華著. −−初版. −−臺北市：五南, 2016.10

面； 公分

ISBN 978-957-11-8834-8（平裝附光碟片）

1. 英語 2. 讀本

805.18 105017028

1XOB

開口就會英國長住用語

作 者 周樹華
發 行 人 楊榮川
總 編 輯 王翠華
企劃主編 溫小瑩、朱曉蘋
責任編輯 吳雨潔
封面設計 吳佳臻
美術設計 吳佳臻

出 版 者 五南圖書出版股份有限公司
地 址：台北市大安區106和平東路二段339號4樓
電 話：(02)2705-5066 傳真：(02)2706-6100
網 址：http://www.wunan.com.tw
電子郵件：wunan@wunan.com.tw
劃撥帳户：01068953
户 名：五南圖書出版股份有限公司

法律顧問 林勝安律師事務所 林勝安律師

出版日期 2016年10月初版一刷

定 價 380元整